# I Always Have

# and

# I Always Will

Alisha Stutson

Published by Purpose Media Publishing, Little Rock, AR



For information, contact:
Purpose Media Publishing
P.O. Box 15561
Little Rock, AR 72231

Printed in the United States of America

Cover design: Alisha Stutson

Please consider requesting that a copy of this book be purchased by your local library system.

Library of Congress Control Number:2024908368

ISBN: 979-8-9900895-1-8

# Table of Contents

# Dedication

I dedicate this book to my husband, Jonathon. We started as best friends and turned our lives into a love story. I am thankful to have you by my side through this journey we call life.

I love you!

"For those of you that are looking for a Scottie in your life, I encourage you to be patient and don't give up hope of finding him. I know he is out there searching for his Abby. One day, you will connect and begin your love story. How do I know you ask? Easy, I married my Scottie."

*Always Be Together – Little Mix*

# CHAPTER 1

## Our Last Field Trip

"Why do my parents have to destroy my life?" Abigail thought to herself as she stared out the window. Everything was going great. Her summer was only days away, and she was looking forward to summer camp and trips with her friends, but all her plans were unraveled after last night's dinner. "How can I tell them that this is our last field trip together?" She murmured to herself.

"Ow!" Abigail spoke sharply, grabbing her forehead. Her head bounced off the window with a thump as Mrs. Mia turned into the San Antonio Christian School parking lot.

"I am sorry. Are you okay?" Mrs. Mia asked.

"I will be fine," Abigail snapped. Her world was crushed by her parents' announcement that they were moving at the end of June. Mr. Arnold was retiring from the military, and had accepted a job offer as a Naval Criminal Investigator in Savannah, GA. Isabella Smith and Abigail had been best friends since pre-k, and she had no idea how to break the news that this would be their last field trip together. "It feels as if it was just yesterday that we were on the playground playing hide and seek," Abigail thought to herself.

"Abigail, I know you are upset, but this move won't be as bad as you are assuming. You will make new friends in no time," Mrs. Mia assured.

"I don't want new friends, nor do I want to move. I am happy and content with my life here. Isabella and I have talked about going to high school together since we were in the sixth grade. I don't understand why Dad can't find a job here," Abigail said as she turned to grab the backpack she filled with snacks and extra clothes for emergencies.

"This is your dad's dream career, and there are no available positions here in this area. We need to support him." Mrs. Mia replied.

"What about my dreams?" Abigail asked abruptly.

"Abigail, we do support your dreams, but you are only 14 years old. You have your entire life ahead of you. Who knows where your dreams are going to take you, but this is an opportunity for him to fulfill his lifelong dream. Can you give it a chance for his happiness?" Mrs. Mia added as a horn came from an impatient parent waiting in line. "We can discuss it more tonight. Call me to let me know when you are leaving Sea World, so I can be here when y'all arrive." Mrs. Mia said, breaking the silence.

"Yes ma'am." Abigail replied.

"Be safe and have fun. I love you," Mrs. Mia called out as Abigail stepped out of the vehicle.

"I love you too." Abigail forced a smile and shut the door. She slung the backpack on her right shoulder and waved to her mom as she pulled away. "We are moving to Savannah, GA."
Abigail rehearsed the lines to herself as she turned to walk into the school.

"Abigail!" Isabella squealed as she slammed the car door behind her and started jogging toward Abigail. Abigail turned just in time to brace herself for the impact of Isabella's hug. "Are you as excited as I am?" She asked as they linked arms and walked up the stairs to enter the school lobby. "A full day of rides, no schoolwork, and of course a day with BJ."

"I am excited about the rides and no schoolwork, but I will leave spending time with BJ up to you," Abigail teased.

"I know one person who wouldn't mind spending the day with you," Isabella stated. Abigail rolled her eyes.

"I have told you multiple times that your brother is just an arrogant boy who likes every girl he meets. I am not interested in him. I am sorry, but he is not my type at all."

"Are you hassling her about Rhett again?" Brooke asked as she walked up next to them.

"She knows he has liked her since her glow-up last summer. Quite frankly no one is your type," Isabella taunted.

"We need to get to homeroom before the bell rings, and we are tardy," Abigail stated, ignoring Isabella's comment. Rhett was Isabella's twin brother. Though they were identical, they had slightly different features. They both had the natural thick, wavy, blonde hair that complemented their olive-toned skin. Rhett kept his hair cut short during the school year but would let it grow out during the summer. Isabella's hair was shoulder length, which fell naturally with the beach waves around her face. They had piercing blue eyes that reminded her of Zac Efron's eyes. His dreamy looks were what drew the girls in like pollen draws-in bees. That was for every girl except Abigail Whittinger. Rhett was taller than Isabella, and his face was fuller than hers. The tardy bell rang as they entered their homeroom class with Mrs. Harper Winthrop.

"Good morning, everyone. When I call your name please raise your hand," Mrs. Winthrop announced after everyone was seated. She picked up a stack of papers from her desk and began to call each student's name out one by one. Everyone in the room had their hands up once she reached the last paper in the stack. "Looks like everyone has turned in their permission slips and we are all good to go. We will begin loading the bus at 9:00 AM, so I will let you visit each other for another thirty minutes if you use your inside voices. But once you start getting too loud, then I will have to resolve to no talking." She sat down at her desk and placed the papers back in a manilla folder. Low murmurs began to fill the classroom as they chatted with their friends in low voices.

"Is your mom still coming as a chaperone?" Isabella asked as she turned to face Brooke.

"Yes. However, I think she is driving there and will meet us at the gate," Brooke answered.

"I am glad my mom didn't volunteer for this trip," Abigail inserted.

"What? Girl, your mom is a blast. I would prefer her out of all our moms," Brooke stated.

"I have never heard you say that you don't want to be around your mother before. Is everything okay?" Isabella questioned.

"Yes. I am just not happy with my parents right now." Abigail replied.

"Out of all the years I have known you, you haven't ever been at odds with them."

"Oh my, they aren't getting a divorce, are they?" Brooke asked in a whisper, leaning close to her.

"What? No," Abigail assured. "I don't want to talk about it right now. I just want to go and have a good time with my friends on our last field trip together."

"Last field trip together?" Isabella asked in a high-pitched tone that made Mrs. Winthrop glare at her.

"Inside voice," Brooke said softly looking over at Isabella.

"Yeah, our last field trip together as eighth graders," Abigail stated, trying to cover up what she said.

"Whew. You scared me. I thought you were telling us you were moving or something," Isabella giggled. Abigail felt bad for lying to them, but she was not about to ruin this field trip. She wanted to wait until the moment was right to tell them, and right now was not the time.

Everyone was sweating and hot after they had waited in line for an hour to enter the park. "We will divide up into groups of 10 to 12 students with one chaperone," Mr. Walters, the principal, called out. The chaperones and teachers stood out from the crowd in a single file line. The parents would have their children and nine other students in their group. After everyone was divided into groups, they set a time to meet back at the gate, and each group departed. Mrs. Cooper, Brooke's mom, was assigned to be the chaperone over Brooke, Rhett, Abigail, Isabella, BJ, Roger, Daniel, Maxine, Dominique, and Heather. "Where are we going first," she asked as she looked over the park's map, which each chaperone was given. "We can start here and go left or right until we finish the entire park."

"Let's ride a water ride to cool off," Roger Green called out.

"There are only two water rides. We have the Journey to Atlantis which is up here on the right, or they have the raft ride, Rio Loco, which is past the Orca stadium on the right as well." The Rio Loco was voted on. Abigail, Rhett, Isabella, BJ, Brooke, and Daniel were the first to board a raft after a twenty-minute wait in line. "Wait for us at the exit gate," Mrs. Cooper called out as their raft rolled down the conveyor belt to be released into the water.

"Yes ma'am," Brooke answered. Everyone waved to their friends who were still waiting for their raft to arrive. As their raft left the conveyer belt, they were led down a stream of white-water caps with small dips. They waved to the bystanders standing on the bridge watching their friends or family as the rafts drifted by underneath them. The raft bounced off the narrow wall, turning slightly with the fast-paced water. The girls would get excited at the small dips in fear of being splashed by water. The narrow walls opened to rapid waters and Brooke squealed as a splash of chilly water came over the side of the raft and drenched her and Daniel. Everyone giggled.

"I am sure that is just a taste of what is to come," BJ said.

"The water is cold," she shivered.

The raft bounced off the black and white poles that were slightly a foot above the water causing it to twirl once more. Abigail and Rhett were now at the mercy of the raging waves that were just ahead. They both peeked around the high backrest of their seat to see what was coming up. "Someone's about to get wet," Daniel teased.

As they came to the big dip, Abigail held her breath. A huge wave of water splashed against the back of their seats and covered them. She let out a high-pitched scream, and everyone in the raft burst with laughter. They were soaked as the raft hit the narrow wall and turned, allowing Brooke and Daniel to be at the mercy of the raging dips of the water. With many small curves and dips, the raft turned and teased with small splashes. Just ahead, the girls began to squeal as the waterfalls came into sight. Isabella and BJ were now on the right with Abigail and Rhett with their backs toward the waves once again.

"Oh NO! We are going to get it!" Isabella screamed. "Turn raft!" she let out with a screech, grabbing the big wheel in the middle of the raft and pulling with all her might as if she was going to turn the raft in her favor. The waterfall roared as they came closer and it splashed Rhett, Isabella, and Daniel as they drifted under it. Everyone laughed as they let out screams from being soaked from head to toe by the cold water. They went through a few more turns and dips without anyone getting splashed. The waters began to calm a little as they approached the conveyor belt, pulling the raft uphill to their exit. Almost all of them were drenched and cooled off as they exited the raft. They grabbed their bags out of the cubby holes where they had placed their belongings at the beginning of the ride. They stood off to the side of the exit gate waiting for the others in their group to arrive.

"While we are waiting, I am going to dry off as much as possible," Abigail said. She pulled out a beach towel from her bag and dried off. She wrapped the towel around her hair and rubbed it between her hands. She looped the damp towel through the loop of her backpack and tied it in a knot so it could air dry. With the band she had on her wrist, she placed her hair in a low ponytail at the nape of her neck. She pulled on her orange baseball cap sporting the Longhorns with the white decal and pulled her hair through the opening gap. She squeezed a portion of sunscreen from the tube and rubbed it over her legs, arms, neck, and face for protection from the sun.

"Why didn't I think to wear a cap to keep the sun out of my eyes?" Brooke inquired. "All I have is my sunglasses, and they can only do so much."

"Maybe you can buy a souvenir cap from one of the gift shops," Daniel suggested.

"That is a great idea. I will buy one when we pass one of the shops," Brooke said, grabbing the sunscreen from Abigail and applying it.

"I may get one as well," Isabella said as she pulled her hair up in a messy bun.

A few moments later, the rest of the group arrived at the exit gate, soaked. Mrs. Cooper retrieved her map from her bag and opened it up. "Where to next?"

"Let's ride the Sting Ray," BJ called out in his country drawl. Billy James Dawson, BJ, has dirty blonde hair, green eyes, light brown freckles on his cheeks, and suntan skin. He preferred to be outside instead of being cooped up in his home. Isabella had a crush on him since the start of their sixth-grade year. He started paying more attention to her after summer camp last year. Her parents did not allow them to date due to them both being too young, but they were a cute pair together. Some of the others didn't want to ride, which was fine with Mrs. Cooper. They stayed back at the exit gate and waited for the others. After everyone had had their thrills on the coaster, they visited the turtle reef to begin making their way around the park.

"Oh my, that smell," Maxine squealed. She and the others pulled their shirts over their nose as the fishy smell was so strong when entering the Penguin encounter. Though the smell was a bit overpowering, the dark, cool air gave them a break from the heat of the sun. A few stood in front of the glass watching the penguins swim and play while the others decided to sit on the seats lined against the back wall to enjoy the scene.

"You know that the penguins mate for life. They return year after year to one another," Rhett explained as he took a seat next to Abigail.

"Are you making that up?" She asked, rolling her eyes at him.

"Nope. Learned in on the Discovery Channel once." Rhett added.

"You watch the Discovery Channel?" Abigail asked.

"No. It happened to be on in a doctor's office waiting room once. There was nothing else to do, so I watched as they explored these loud, stinky, flightless birds. It was quite fascinating, to be honest." He answered.

"Shocks me that you even gave it a second glance," she teased.

"It reminded me of Happy Feet the movie. You know, with Mumble who is trying to get Gloria's attention, but he can't sing a note to save his life. Then he is cast out by the elder penguins." He continued.

"Yes, I remember watching it when I was younger," she said.

"You are my Gloria, and I will keep dancing around you until I get your attention." He said.

"Rhett, you will waste your time. You are a friend to me, and that is all we will ever be."

"You say that now, but just wait until you come around one day, then you would see that we are meant to be mates for life. Just like Gloria and Mumble." He winked at her with a smile and walked over to where BJ and Isabella were looking through the glass.

Once everyone was cooled off and ready to move on, they rode the Steel Eel, which is Abigail and Isabella's favorite ride. It is a hyper coaster that brings you up to a fifteen-story, vertical drop, and periods of weightless moments. They held their hands in the air screaming at every drop and turn. They were almost voiceless after they rode it for the fifth time in a row. "I saw you and Rhett talking in the penguin encounter. Anything I should know about?" Isabella teased.

"He was telling me about how penguins mate for life. That he will be like Mumble off Happy Feet, and dance around me until I take him as my mate." Abigail replied.

"He is so quirky," Isabella giggled.

"I know, right." Abigail answered.

"I don't know how he picks up girls with all the weird lines he uses." Isabella continued.

"I am not going to fall for those piercing blue eyes of his. He forgets that I have seen all the tricks he has played on other girls this past year. I refuse to be a victim to his games." Abigail said.

"I think it would be different with you. He has liked you for as long as I can remember." Isabella noted.

"He just wants what he can't have, and that messes with his ego knowing that I am not giving in." Abigail replied.

"He doesn't try to win over other girls. They just come to him, and he only gives them a week or two of his time. Once he gets tired of their clinginess with him, he cuts them loose. That only takes a week or two, and then on to the next one. The only reason he flirts with girls in front of you is to make you jealous," Isabella explained.

"There is nothing to be jealous about. I don't see Rhett any other way." They walked through the park experiencing the fun thrill rides and awesome animal exhibits the park had to offer, and ended the day with the Orca Whale show. Abigail called her mom once they were headed to load on the buses to return to the school.

Everyone was so exhausted that the bus ride home was quiet. They arrived at the school at 6:45 PM. Abigail climbed into the backseat, and the cool leather felt amazing on the warmth of her sunbaked skin. She closed her eyes and leaned her head back on the headrest.

"Did you enjoy your time?" Mrs. Mia asked as they pulled out of the parking lot.

"Yes ma'am. I am totally exhausted now," she said with a rough, raspy voice.

"What happened to your voice?" Mrs. Mia asked.

"I believe I left it on the Steel Eel." Abigail replied.

Mrs. Mia giggled, "Ahh. Did you beat your record of rides?"

"Nope, we are still at 10 and holding. We only rode it five times in a row today. We didn't want to take away others' time at the park."

"You two would probably ride it from open to close if you had your way," Mrs. Mia joked.

"I guess we won't be able to find out, since this will be our last trip to Sea World together," Abigail snapped.

"Just because we are moving doesn't mean we won't see them ever again," Mrs. Mia stated, glancing at her in the review mirror.

"I guess we will have to see." Abigail said.

"I know you are upset, and the news was unexpected. It wasn't like we had this planned. This job offer is really good for your father, and it came at the right time for his retirement. It will take time for all of us to adjust to our new schedules, get to know the new area, and meet new people." She paused with a sigh not knowing what words could console her daughter's breaking heart. "Did you tell the others?"

"I don't think ruining our last field trip together would be a great idea," she answered as she swiped a fallen tear from her face. Her heart was crushed by the thought of leaving everyone she grew up with.

"I can make dinner plans tomorrow night at the house, and you can tell them then. I will call the parents to let them know in advance. Does that sound like a plan?" Mrs. Mia asked.

"Sure. I have to tell them sooner or later." Abigail replied.

"I will start the calls after dinner," Mrs. Mia said as they pulled into the garage. They stepped out of the car and entered the house.

"I am not hungry. Can I just shower, and call it a night, please?" Abigail pleaded.

"Are you sure? I made your favorite blackened salmon with sautéed veggies." Mrs. Mia pressed on.

"Thanks, but I think I ate way too much at the park." Abigail answered.

"I will save you a plate and you can eat it for lunch tomorrow." Mrs. Mia concurred.

"Thank you. Good night," Abigail said as she made her way down the hall to her room. When she entered her room she tossed her bag on the floor and shut the door behind her. She fell across her bed, and tears began to flow down her face. She had held them in all day, and now there was no reason to stop them.

*Don't You Forget About Me – Simple Minds*

# CHAPTER 2

## We Are Moving

Abigail was not ready to see the sunbeam through her window. She wished she could just make everything go back to normal. Back to Wednesday evening when her life was booming, and her only worry was planning fun trips with her best friend, Isabella, for the summer. Now her life was being ripped up and moved to Savannah, GA. Where she knew no one, and her friends would be hundreds of miles away. "Enough of this torture. I have to do something to get my mind off of it," she said to herself. She got dressed in some comfortable clothes, put her earbuds, pressed play on her playlist, and started cleaning her room. When she felt angry, stressed, or overwhelmed about anything, cleaning and music was the only therapy that seemed to help her cope with the situation. She scrubbed and cleaned everything until it was spotless, and her room smelled like it was full of lemons. Still feeling the heaviness on her chest, she continued her cleaning to other areas of the house.

She was scrubbing the baseboards in the hallway jamming out to 'Shake It Off' by Taylor Swift when Mrs. Mia came out of the kitchen. She leaned against the door frame and watched Abigail shake to the music as she wiped down the baseboard. She knew the move was tearing her apart, but she had enough faith that Abigail was strong enough to overcome the obstacles that lay ahead and would make new friends very easily.

"AH!" Abigail squealed and pulled the earbuds from her ears. Shake It Off lyrics filled the hallway through her earbuds.

"I am sorry. I didn't mean to startle you. I know cleaning and music are your therapy, and I didn't want to disturb you." Mrs.Mia said.

"Mom, my heart is racing. How long have you been standing there?" Abigail asked.

"Not long," she answered as she stood up straight.

"I am just cleaning the house and getting it ready for tonight," Abigail stated as she wrapped the earbuds around her neck and let them hang inside her shirt. She paused the music and went back to cleaning.

"You know spring has come and gone, and I clean the baseboards every time I mop so I am pretty sure they aren't that dirty," Mrs. Mia teased.

"Maybe so, but this helps me." Abigail said.

"I have the leftover salmon and veggies heating up if you are hungry." Mrs. Mia replied.

Abigail had ignored her growling stomach for the last hour or two. She had skipped breakfast and was feeling hungry. Once she got into her therapy cleaning, it was best to continue until she felt the release in her chest or until she had cleaned the entire house. She looked over the baseboards, and there was only one short wall left to do. "I am almost done, and I will wash my hands to eat." Abigail said.

"I will fix your plate for you." Mrs. Mia turned and disappeared back into the kitchen. Abigail placed an earbud in her left ear, and pressed play.

She entered the kitchen moments later and sat down at the table by Mrs. Mia. "This looks delicious. Thank you."

"You are welcome." Mrs. Mia said.

They sat and ate, enjoying their small talk. Neither one mentioned the elephant in the room. "I have called all the parents and we plan to eat at six o'clock. I am sure some will arrive a little early. I was thinking that I could make lasagna with creamed corn, and a green salad for the side. Does that sound good?" Mrs.Mia started.

"Can we have some garlic bread as well?" Abigail asked.

"Of course, and a peach cobbler for dessert. Good?" Mrs. Mia replied.

"Yes ma'am. Can I help?" Abigail added.

"I wouldn't have it any other way," Mrs. Mia said with a smile. "I will put the lasagna in the oven at five o'clock. It will take about forty-five minutes to cook, and we can start the sides when it is almost done. We can set the table now and it will be ready. We will just have to place the food items in the center when everything is ready to go."

"I can wash the veggies now, that way, the lettuce will be dry, and not soggy," Abigail stated before taking a bite of her salmon.

"Great idea, we can make the peach cobbler if you like. We can heat it up once everyone is ready for dessert." Mrs.Mia continued.

"Sure. Keeping my hands busy helps my mind not to focus on the reason they are coming over." Abigail took her last bite of salmon. She was about to stand up to go clean her plate when Mrs. Mia grabbed her.

"I know this is all very hard on you, and I truly wish I could take all the pain and hurt you are feeling away. It is not good to keep it bottled up inside. You know I am always here if you want to talk, and I am saving a gallon of butter pecan ice cream for when you are ready."

"Thank you, Mom. I know you are here and I will take you up on that offer. Just give me some time to get my thoughts and feelings in check first." Abigail answered.

"I understand." She gave her hand a little squeeze and released it. "You want to watch a movie while the cobbler is baking? I can set the timer to cut the oven off once it is done to keep it from getting burnt." Mrs.Mia added.

"Sure, did you have anything picked out?" Abigail asked as she rinsed off her dish and placed it in the dishwasher.

"How about Freaky Friday the 2000 version?" Mrs. Mia asked as she walked over to the sink to clean her dish.

"Sounds perfect," Abigail agreed.

They got busy in the kitchen getting everything ready for dinner. They set the table, had the pot warmer in place for the lasagna in the center of the table and the places marked for the side dishes.

"I believe that is all. The cobbler is in the oven, and the timer is set," Mrs. Mia said.

"I will pop some popcorn for us to munch on." Abigail said, and then grabbed a large pottery cream bowl with blue small spots with the words "POPCORN IS FOR SHARING" written on the wide, cream rim of the bowl. It was their bowl that they filled with popcorn for movie and game nights. They got situated and comfortable with blankets on the couch, and watched the movie.

Everyone gathered around the large dining table enjoying the meal that Mrs. Mia had prepared. Laughter bounced off the walls as they shared stories of their SeaWorld experience from the last day of school. Abigail glanced around the table soaking in every smile, laugh, and face that surrounded her. This would be the last time they would probably have everyone over in this house. Her heart was heavy as she blinked back the tears that were about to escape her eyes. *This isn't fair,* she thought to herself, slightly shaking her head to fight back her emotions.

"Are you okay?" Isabella asked, looking over at Abigail.

"Yeah. I was just lost in my thoughts for a moment," she answered.

"I can see that. Are you thinking of some summer trips for us to do this summer?" Isabella pressed on.

"I haven't given it much thought." Abigail answered.

"Are you sure you are okay?" Isabella asked.

"Yes. Why are asking me that?" Abigail asked, pushing her leftover salad around with her fork.

"Normally you have lots of ideas for us to do during the summer before we even get out of school," Isabella answered.

"That is true. Last year you had our entire summer filled with activities in mid-May," Brooke agreed.

"I guess I have lost my touch," Abigail said as she laid her fork down on her plate and placed her hands in her lap.

"If everyone is finished with their meal. We can gather in the den," Mrs. Mia stated as she stood and picked up her dishes. One by one everyone stood and collected their dishes, following her to the kitchen. "You men can go and get settled, I believe we can handle the rest."

"I am not going to argue with that," Mr. Arnold, Abigail's dad teased. He placed his dishes on the bar by the sink. "Well, you heard her guys. Let's grab a cup of coffee first."

"Now that sounds like a plan," Mr. Cooper said. They each grabbed a cup of coffee as the girls helped the ladies put away the leftovers, and Mrs. Mia loaded the dishwasher.

Everyone had taken their seats when Abigail entered the den, leaving the only open seat next to Rhett on the coach. She sat down and made eye contact with Isabella as if asking her to get her out of sitting there, but Isabella just gave her a teasing wink. Of course, she was happy to be sitting by BJ, so she wasn't worried about Abigail being uncomfortable sitting next to the boy who contiuously annoyed her. She was playing cupid trying to get the two together anyway. Their secret conversation with their eyes and motions was interrupted when Mr. Arnold sat his coffee cup down and began to speak.

"We asked to see you here tonight because we have some news that we need to share." Everyone gave him their undivided attention. Abigail began to fiddle with her hands to keep her nerves at bay, and did not look up from her lap. "We have all become like family over the years that we have lived here, so there will be no easy way to say what I am about to tell you. Therefore, I am going to rip the band-aid off, and just tell you." Everyone looked over at each other in confusion, not understanding what is about to be said. "I have taken a job offer in Savannah, GA, and we will be moving there at the end of June." Oh my and gasps filled the air. "Just because we are moving doesn't mean we won't see each other anymore. We will just not be able to visit as often as we do now." He held Mrs. Mia's hand.

"I surely wasn't expecting that," Rhett said. "I was thinking you were going to tell us that y'all were expecting or something." Laughter filled the room, except for Abigail and Isabella. Isabella looked up at Abigail and their eyes met. Tears began to stream down their faces. Abigail stood up from where she sat, walked over and kneeled down in front of her, and they embraced each other.

"I am sorry. I wanted to tell you, but I didn't find out until Thursday night at dinner. I wanted us to enjoy our field trip, and there wasn't a good time to tell you," Abigail whispered.

"I don't know how I can start high school without you." They squeezed each other even tighter, and Brooke came over and joined in on the group hug.

"Girls, we will plan for you to see each other as often as possible." Mrs. Mia assured them.

"You can Facetime and text every day," Mrs. Smith, Rhett and Isabella's mom, stated.

"Yeah, just because you aren't going to be living close by doesn't mean you cannot communicate or stay in touch," Mrs. Cooper, Brooke's mom, said.

"It isn't the same," Isabella whispered.

"I know, but your friendship is strong enough to see you through this," Mrs. Smith comforted as she stood behind them with her hands on Isabella's shoulders.

"Y'all can spend as much time together as you would like before we leave," Mr. Arnold spoke up.

"We could use all the help we can get packing up our things. We are taking volunteer work for anyone who would like to assist in our moving sale, which we are having in two weeks."

BJ and Rhett both agreed to help in any way possible.

Everyone sat for the next few hours discussing the move that was to come in just three short weeks. It was approaching 10:30 PM when Mr. Dawson said it was time for them to head home. It was like a domino effect as the others started following them to the door.

"May I stay over a few nights every week until y'all leave," Isabella asked as she said her goodbyes.

"Of course, and you can start on Monday night if that is fine with your parents," Mrs. Mia said, smiling at Mrs.Smith.

"I am sure that will be better than you sitting at home and pondering the days to come," Mr. Smith agreed. The girls grabbed each other in a group hug and squeezed each other tight. The boys took turns hugging Abigail and telling her they were going to miss seeing her around. Rhett's hug lasted a little longer than BJ's, and Abigail stood in his embrace as long as he wanted. She knew that though she didn't like him in the manner that Isabella wished, it was more like a brother hugging his sister who was going off to college goodbye.

The moving sale was a hit. They were able to sell all the big items, and a lot of the items they didn't want to take with them. Isabella, Brooke, and the boys were over as much as possible assisting with getting everything ready for the move. The moving boxes were stacked up nice and neat in the uhaul truck. Their hanging clothes were wrapped in bags with ten items of clothing to each, and hung on wires that were stretched across from one side to another side of the truck bed. It was their last night and they would be staying in a hotel since there were no beds in the home. The Smiths asked them out to dinner for their last night in town. They decided to meet at *The Republic of Texas* restaurant on the riverwalk at seven o'clock. It was now 4:30 PM and they were making their last runs through the house to make sure nothing was left behind. They all looked back at the house from the front lawn with their arms wrapped around each other. They looked over the home that had sheltered them over the past ten years. "It was a nice place to call home," Mr. Arnold said.

*It's Nice to Have a Friend– Taylor Swift*

# CHAPTER 3

## Freshman Year - 2011-12

Savannah and San Antonio are alike in some ways- with lots of fun activities and extraordinary historic tours, but it still wasn't home. Just moving here a few weeks before school didn't give Abigail much time to meet anyone. She barely had enough time to settle in, get used to her parents' new work schedules, and such. It was nice having a pool in the backyard, but swimming alone wasn't much fun. It made her miss Isabella and the others even more. They would video chat as much as possible. Though it wasn't the same as being there, it helped more than not seeing them at all. Her alarm was announcing the beginning of her first day of school. She hit the snooze button but didn't budge to get out of bed. Her phone dinged with a text notification from Isabella.

"Missing you! Wish we could start this day together. I know it will be harder for you today since everything and everyone will be new. You are beautiful, smart, and headstrong. You've got this! Who knows, maybe you will meet the one to finally steal your attention from your books and sports. JK. Truly wish I was there with you. Call me as soon as you can! Can't wait to get all the details! Have a great day!"

"It would be so much easier with you here with me. Thank you for the encouraging text. Will call you as soon as I get home. Have a great day!" Abigail replied. She laid her phone down beside her on the bed. *I thought Isabella and I would be starting high school together, and it would be easier with her beside me. Starting at a new school, where I know no one, is going to be tough.* She thought to herself. Abigail lay in bed wishing she could find an excuse to miss school today, but with a mom as a nurse that is nearly impossible to do. A knock on her door jolted her back from the thoughts. "Time to get up. You don't want to be late for your first day," Mr. Arnold chimed, as he passed to go downstairs.

"Yes sir. I'm awake," she answered. Although her feet had yet to move much less touch the floor. She lay there for a few more minutes staring at the white ceiling, coercing herself to get up. She rose and pulled the covers back and placed her feet on the floor. If only the butterflies in her stomach would settle down. She looked over at her clock which displayed 6:15 AM. Normally she would have more time to sleep in but not today. Her dad was going to take her for her first day. She pushed off the bed, grabbed the outfit she picked out the night before, and off to the bathroom she went.

Abigail stood looking at herself in the mirror. She straightened her fine, straight, dirty blonde hair and pulled half of it back with a small clip. She made minor adjustments to the baby hairs that were around the frame of her face. She gave herself a look over once more and sighed, "I guess this will have to do." She headed downstairs to have breakfast. When she came around the corner to the kitchen, she saw Mr. Arnold sitting at the large island drinking his morning cup of coffee and finishing up his eggs and bacon. She tossed her backpack on a seat next to him. "I cooked you breakfast but wasn't sure if you wanted coffee or orange juice," he said as she grabbed a plate from the cabinet.

"Thank you. Orange juice will be fine," she smiled. She fixed a small plate and poured herself a glass of juice.

"We need to leave in 15 minutes, so we will be on time," he stated as she sat down on the other side of him.

"Yes sir. That is plenty of time to eat and brush my teeth," she answered before taking the first bite of her eggs.

"Are you ready for your first day of high school?" Mr. Arnold asked.

"Not really. I am so scared. What if no one likes me?" Abigail answered.

"I don't see that happening," he assured her as he rinsed off his dishes and placed them in the dishwasher. "You are beautiful and kind. I am sure you will have no problem with making new friends on your first day."

"We will see," she moaned as she finished the last bite of her bacon. She picked up her dishes and placed them in the dishwasher. "Going to brush my teeth and will be down in a jiffy." She ran upstairs to her bathroom, brushed, and flossed her teeth. She came down just as Mr. Arnold was placing his last needed items on his belt.

"Are you ready?" He asked as he grabbed his keys.

"As ready as I can be." She picked up her backpack and they walked out the door.

The sun was shining brightly, and it was already 70 degrees. Her dad turned on the air conditioner to cool the car, and the radio to break the silence on the way to school. They both loved listening to jazz or instrumental songs to soothe them when riding. Abigail gazed out the window listening to the saxophone and guitar picking coming out of the speakers. She leaned back in her seat and let the beat carry her anxious thoughts away. Moments later, they arrived at H.V. Jenkins High School, and just that fast the butterflies returned in her stomach. She looked at Mr. Arnold with a nervous smile as she unlocked her seat belt.

"You will be fine. I know that when I arrive home you will be telling me all about your day and your new friends," he assured her with a smile. She leaned over and hugged his neck.

"Bye Daddy. I love you." She said.

"I love you, too." Mr. Arnold replied.

"Have a good day!" he called out as she was closing the door. He watched her as long as he could till the parents behind him honked as if to say, 'Move it'. He pulled away with one last glance at his not-so-little girl entering the school.

Abigail walked into the office to get her schedule for her classes. She was greeted by Ms. Charlotte Richardson, the guidance counselor. She had beautiful dark green eyes and a nice complexion. Her long, bouncy black hair was styled with the layers that framed her face, which gave her a youthful look.

"Good morning. How can I help you?" she asked as she looked up from the paperwork on her desk. Her smile was very welcoming and made it easy to approach her.

"I am Abigail Whittinger, and I need to get my schedule, please," Abigail answered.

"I have everything here for you," she stated as she picked up a folder from the right side of her desk. "Miranda," she called out to a girl standing behind her, filing some folders away.

"Yes, Ms. Charlotte," she said as she laid the files down on top of the filing cabinet and walked behind her chair.

"This is Abigail Whittinger," she said. Abigail smiled. "Abigail, this is Miranda Johnson. She is the office assistant in the mornings," Miranda returned the smile. She was slightly taller than Abigail. With a natural tight curly blonde hair, blue eyes, and a nice tan. She must have been outside in the sun more than Abigail. "Would you mind showing her to homeroom?" she continued as she handed Miranda Abigail's schedule.

"Sure," Miranda agreed and took the schedule.

"Have a good day, Abigail. I am here if you need anything," Ms. Charlotte said with a smile and went back to work.

"Where are you from?" Miranda inquired as they strolled down the crowded, noisy hallway.

"San Antonio, Texas," Abigail responded.

"I was born here in Savannah, so I know most of the freshmen," she assured her. "Although I am a little nervous about starting high school. It gives my stomach butterflies just thinking about it," Miranda said, rubbing her stomach. "I am sure your nerves are worse than mine since being here is new for you." She continued. Abigail gave her a shy nod. "Don't worry, we can get through our first day together. I mean if you would like to," she suggested as she tilted her head to Abigail some locks of her curls fell off her shoulder.

"Yes. That would be great," Abigail replied with relief, knowing that she would have someone to help her cope with her anxiety, which was making her nauseated.

"You don't talk much do you," Miranda teased. Abigail gave her a smirk. "Well, here we are. Let me see… your home room class is with Margaret Rozier, and your first period is English with Mr. Allen Hall. Second is Algebra with Mr. Richard Walters, third is World History with Mr. Joseph Prestridge, fourth is P.E. with Coach Wilkins, fifth is Spanish with Mrs. Doris Harris, sixth is Art with Ms. Paula West, and you will finish out the day in Biology with Mr. Bill Nichols. So, it looks like we have Algebra, P.E., and Spanish together," she said as she handed Abigail the schedule. "We have lunch between the 2nd and 3rd period, so if you would like we can go to lunch together," Miranda added.

"Yes," Abigail answered, looking over her schedule.

"Well, we have reached Mrs. Rozier's class. The teachers have their names engraved in brass plates above their door. It makes it a lot easier to find your class that way," she smiled and pointed to Mrs. Rozier's nameplate above her door. "I will see you meet up with you before we head to second period," she said, waving as she started going down the hallway to her 1st period class. Abigail waved back.

Abigail stepped into her classroom and almost everyone had already taken their seats. Mrs. Rozier was sitting at her desk to the right of the room facing the children. She was very petite with chin-length, shiny, black hair, styled with curls. Her skin tone was light brown, and she had beautiful hazel-green eyes. She met Abigail as she entered the classroom. "Good morning. I am Mrs. Margaret Rozier," she greeted her with a smile that calmed her nerves just a bit.

"Abigail Whittinger," Abigail answered with a soft tone and shy smile.

"I have assigned you a seat. On your desk, you will find the papers you will need to take home to be filled out by your parents or guardians. They will need to be returned tomorrow along with your school fees," she led Abigail to the third row of desks. "You are the 4th one back in front of Scottie Harmon," she said, still pointing toward her seat.

"Thank you," Abigail said as she walked past her toward the desk. Abigail took her seat and placed her backpack down beside her on the floor. She jumped as the bell rang to announce the start of her first day as a freshman. *I need to calm down,* she thought to herself as she took a deep breath to calm her fast-beating heart.

"Are you okay?" someone whispered from behind her. She turned to acknowledge the person behind. Her eyes met a cute, brown curly-haired boy, with brown eyes that had a hint of green around the iris. He resembled her celebrity crush Cameron Boyce, without the adorable freckles. “I saw you jump when the bell rang,” he explained.

“Oh, yes. I am fine. I just wasn't expecting the bell to be that loud,” she giggled.

“I’m Scottie,” he returned with a smile.

"Abigail." She could feel the heat begin to rise from her cheeks to her ears. She twirled in her seat to face the front of the classroom. Hoping he didn't see her blushing.

Mrs. Rozier stood in the front of the classroom resting against her desk. “Good morning, everyone.”

“Good morning,” the class responded.

“I am going to confirm that everyone is present by taking attendance. Then I will take you to the assigned locker where you can store your items during the day,” she stated as she opened a spiral black book, and began calling each student out one by one, as they replied with a “here”. Once everyone was accounted for, she laid the black book down on her desk and stood up. “Everyone, grab your belongings and follow me.” They all stood up and followed her quietly to the hallway. The lockers were on the left and right sides of the hallway, in between the classroom doors. “If you look at the lockers you will see numbers on them. On the top right-hand corner of your paper are your locker number and the combination is underneath it. You will need to memorize the combination to get access to your locker,” she explained as she stood by the door to the classroom. “Now go and put your belongings in your locker. Everything else can stay in your locker. Remain quiet to respect the other classes around you,” she continued as she patiently waited for them all to return to place their items in the locker and then return to class.

Abigail made her way over to the lockers. She looked for number fifteen, and once she located it, she was excited to see it was a top locker not having to bend down to get to it. She waited for the girl below her to place her things and then stepped up to enter the combination. Scottie was standing at locker number thirteen, which was right next to her. "So, you are new here, huh?" he asked her as he placed his items in his locker.

"Yes," she answered softly.

"Where are you from?" He continued.

"San Antonio, Texas." Abigail replied.

"Oh wow. I have always wanted to go there to see the Alamo, and of course, go to FIESTA Six Flags," he joked, trying to ease her nerves.

"I have been to both of course and SeaWorld," she giggled, still fighting with the combination lock.

"Sea World huh? I have never been there either. I thought the only one was in Florida," he said, placing his last pack of paper in the locker before shutting the locker.

"Yeah, it is fun. My favorite ride is the EEL," she stated, now getting agitated because she can't figure out the mechanism of the lock.

"Here, let me help you," he gestured as he moved in to work the lock for her. "What is the combination?"

"05-25-10," she replied.

"You have to turn it right two full times past zero and then stop at 05. Turn left past 05 and stop at 25. Then turn right to 10 and push up to open the locker." He explained.

"You made that look so easy," she said as she moved in to place her things in the locker.

"After class, we can try it again to make sure you can open it," he offered.

"Okay. Thank you," she said, unpacking her backpack into the locker.

"No Problem at all," Scottie whispered and turned to go back to class.

After they were dismissed from homeroom, Abigail and Scottie went to the lockers to allow Abigail time to practice opening her locker before 1$^{st}$ period. She was mumbling the instructions that Scottie had given her to open the locker, but instead of turning it past the zero two times she only passed it once, so the locker wouldn't open. She began to feel anxious again, not able to open something that looked so simple.

"It's okay. Try it again and remember you must pass the zero twice before stopping at your first number," Scottie said. She twirled the lock to clear it and began again.

"Turn right two times past zero. One, two, and now stop at five. Turn left past zero and stop at 25," she mumbled as she was easing to a stop on the 25$^{th}$ dial of the lock. "Now turn right to ten," she stopped at ten and lifted the handle on the locker, and it opened.

"You did it!" Scottie cheered with a smile.

"Thank you," she smirked.

"Hello there," Miranda called as she walked up to Abigail's locker. "How was homeroom?"

"It went better than I expected," she sighed with relief. "I wouldn't have been able to get in my locker without his help," she answered, pointing over to Scottie.

"Hey Scottie," Miranda greeted with a smile.

"Y'all know each other?" Abigail asked.

"Yeah. We have been going to school together since the 1st grade," Miranda answered. Scottie shook his head in agreement. "Scottie, what do you have for 1st period?" she inquired.

"PE," he replied cheerfully.

"You sound more excited than I would be," Abigail teased.

"I love PE and sports," he returned with a smile.

"Ah, huh. I love to play volleyball, but I am not so sure about the rest that comes with PE. Getting all sweaty, stinky, and then going to classes the rest of the day," Abigail giggled. "Not in my category of fun." She shut her locker and turned to Miranda.

"So are you ready to head to our next class." Miranda nudged. "We don't want to be late."

"Sure," Abigail answered.

"Hey Scottie, you want to meet up with us at lunch?" Miranda asked.

"Sure, that sounds good to me," he said as he closed his locker.

"See you then," she called out as she and Abigail headed down the hall.

"Boy, what happened to you?" Miranda inquired as they walked three doors down to math class.

"What do you mean?" Abigail inquired.

"You were so quiet that I could barely get more than two words from you this morning, and now look at you having full conversations," Miranda teased.

"I was just nervous this morning and didn't know how to act or how everyone would accept me as a new girl at school. You and Scottie have made me feel comfortable. It eased my nerves and I feel welcome. I was able to let my guard down. You know?" she explained.

"Oh, I know what you mean. I felt the same way when I first moved here. My stomach was in knots until I made friends, and then it was as if I was here all along."

"Yeah, that is exactly it," Abigail agreed.

"Here is Mr. Hall's class." Miranda pointed to a door open on the left where a tall slender man stood with his glasses resting on the tip of his nose. His peppered gray and black hair was combed back in a feathering style to the left side of his face. His green eyes gleamed at them over the rim of his glasses "Good morning," he smiled as they paused in front of his room.

"Morning," they greeted.

"Ok, I will see you in 2nd period," Miranda stated as she headed down the hall.

Abigail took a seat in the second row- far to the back of the room. The bell rang to announce the start of 1st period. Mr. Hall closed the door and walked over to his desk. "Good morning class. We will begin this year by reading Fahrenheit 451 by Ray Bradbury. You will need to check it out at the school or public library, whichever works best for you. We will begin reading tomorrow morning, so make sure you come prepared. Here is a list of the books that we will be reading this year so that you can get a head start if you would like."

Abigail took the paper that was passed back to her. Her eyes scanned the list:

*1. Farenheit 451 by Ray Bradbury*

*2. Romeo and Juliet by William Shakespear*

*3. The Great Gatsby by F. Scott Fitzgerald*

*4. The Outsiders by S.E. Hinton*

*5. Pride and Prejudice by Jane Austen*

*6. The Giver by Lois Lowry*

A slight curve appeared in the corners of her mouth as she saw her favorite book was listed at number five. *I'm going to love this class,* she thought.

Mr. Hall had each of them tell of their favorite book and the reason it made their list. It helped ease everyones nerves and passed the time, because the bell rang to dismiss first period. She met up with Miranda out in the hallway.

"Good morning girls," Mr. Walter greeted them. He was standing just inside the doorway of the classroom greeting everyone as they came in. He was short, and stubby. He had a small bald spot on the top of his head that shined like a ballroom dance floor after being polished, with black and gray hair that was trimmed short on the sides. His glasses couldn't hide his pretty blue eyes.

"Have a seat anywhere you would like. I have placed your math books on the desk for you. Have a seat and we will start discussions once the bell rings."

Abigail and Miranda chose seats next to one another in the second and third row- in the fourth seat back from the front.

The second hour went by quickly and before they knew it the bell rang for lunch. They met at the lockers and headed to the cafeteria. It was a large room with lots of round tables that had six chairs each. After picking through the line of food, they sat and ate by a large window in the back of the room. They talked about their first periods and asked Abigail about San Antonio. She told them about all the things she loved to do, and about the friends she had to leave behind. The bell rang for 3rd Period to begin, and they all put away their trays and headed back to the 9th-grade wing. The first day went by fast, and before Abigail knew it the final bell was ringing to end her first day of school.

The buses were lined up in a row with kids boarding. All the bus drivers had placed their names on the door of the bus to let them know which bus they were to board. She came down to the third bus, where she found her bus driver's name, Mr. Carpenter, on the door.

“Hello, I am Abigail. I live on Van Drive. We just moved there in June,” she introduced herself to the bus driver. Mr. Carpenter was slim, and from the length of his legs, he had to be tall. He had brown hair that was hidden by a baseball cap. Abigail caught a glimpse of his green eyes before he put on his shades.

“Hello there, Abigail. Welcome to Savannah. Hope we have made a good impression on you so far,” he smiled.

“Yes sir,” she returned with a smile.

“Have a seat, and I will have you home shortly.”

Abigail found an empty window seat and sat down. She smiled as everyone passed her to sit with their friends. She didn't mind because she wanted a little time to herself on the ride home. She smiled and she thought to herself *Dad and Isabella were right; today wasn't so bad, and I have two new friends* as she gazed out the window.

# CHAPTER 4

## Labor Day Weekend

The first few weeks of school were not so bad. She still missed everyone, and they spoke on the phone as often as she could. She and Scottie were becoming close. He lived only a block away and would ride his bike over to her house. Not long after they settled in, Mr. Arnold had taken the shed in the backyard and turned it into a game room for them to have a place to go after school. It had electricity so there was a window unit, to help keep it cool on hot summer days, and a mini fridge filled with all the drinks they could drink. He built a small bathroom equipped with a shower, toilet, and sink. A bar with cabinets that held their snacks, and a sink. They had a hockey air table, a pool table, and even a TV setup with the XBOX One Kinect, a DVD player, and cable. They spent most of their time together in the game room.

It was Labor Day weekend, and their parents were planning a get-together, so they all could get to know one another better. Miranda was coming over to spend the entire weekend with her. She was so thrilled to have her over for the weekend. She pulled every board game she could find from the top of her closet and brought it out to the game room. Her parents had approved for them to stay the night in the building instead of the house. Mr. Arnold helped her bring over the sheets, blankets, and pillows for the pullout bed in the loveseat. They had two-way communication handheld devices (walkie-talkies) for communicating back and forth with her parents and in case of emergencies as well. This kept them from having to go back and forth from the house, and her parents from having to yell across the yard. "The pizza is here," Mr. Arnold called over the device.

"On my way," she responded. She ran to grab the pizza and a few good movies to watch when they were done playing games.

"I am headed back out Dad," she hollered as she made her way to the back door, balancing the movies and pizza.

He came into the kitchen, "I stocked the fridge with drinks, and made sure that you have snacks for the night. If y'all need anything just give us a shout. Your mom will be in at seven tonight if she doesn't have to pull a double," he informed her as he held the door open for her.

"Thank you. Just tell Miranda to come on back when she gets here," she said as she crossed the yard.

"Sure thing!" He replied before closing the door.

Abigail was getting out the plates when Miranda came through the door.

"Hey, your dad said to come on back. Wow! You have everything set up nice," she said as she sat her bag down and took a glance.

"Thanks. I didn't know what you would want to do, so I brought some board games and movies from the house for when we get exhausted from Just Dance," Abigail explained.

"We are going to have so much fun this weekend!" Miranda screamed joyfully.

"I know right? Three days together and no school! So, what do you want to do first?" Abigail added.

"How about a game of Monopoly, and then we can play Just Dance till our bodies cannot take it anymore," Miranda suggested.

"That sounds perfect!" Abigail said and pulled out the Monopoly game and started setting up a small round table that Mr. Arnold brought in for them to eat and play board games on. Mrs. Mia checked in on them when she came in from work. They played a game of Monopoly, a couple of games of pool and air hockey, and hours of Just Dance, and ended the night with a shower and a movie.

Saturday morning, Mrs. Mia called over the walkie-talkies to see if they would want to go with her to the store to grab the items needed for the gathering. They said yes and got dressed. They made up the bed and cleaned up the popcorn and drinks from the night before. And when they were down, they went over to the house. Mrs. Mia was finishing up her list of items to buy, and Mr. Arnold was finishing up breakfast.

"Good morning," he greeted them as they came in.

"Good morning," they answered.

"So how was your night? Did you go to bed at a decent hour?" He teased them knowing that was not the case. A decent hour for him is at 9:00 PM. They looked at one another, giggled and shook their heads.

"No sir," they replied.

"That figures," he chuckled.

"Are you girls ready to go assist me with getting the last few items?" Mrs. Mia asked.

"Yes ma'am," Abigail responded.

"Let's get to it then," she said, grabbing her notepad and pen. "We have a lot to do before others get here tonight."

"I am going out to mow, straighten up the yard, and get the fire pit ready for s'mores," Mr. Arnold said as he finished the last bite of his raisin bran.

"Oh, I need to add the s'more items to my list. Thank you for reminding me," Mrs. Mia commented as she jotted down the items.

"That is what I am here for," he said, placing his empty dishes in the dishwasher. "Be careful. See you guys when you get back." Out the door, he went to start his list of things to do.

"Got it. Okay, girls let's go," Mrs. Mia said as she led them to the garage door.

They were only gone for two hours. When they arrived home, Mr. Arnold was finishing up his weed-eating around the fence. He had mowed, put up the lights over the seating area for the guests, placed torches around the yard filled with mosquito repellent oil, and cleaned the grill to barbecue. He also had the croquet game all set up to play. It looked nice. All that was left was taking the cover off the fire pit and stacking the wood. He then went inside and helped Mrs. Mia prepare the food for dinner. It was set for everyone to be there for seven, but the others started arriving around five. The women went to the kitchen to bring the food they had prepared, and the guys went out to help with the grilling, which meant talking and eating the food they were grilling. Around six, Mr. Arnold lit the torches and started the fire pit. The weather was perfect, with a nice breeze blowing.

They ate around seven o'clock. The men cooked the chicken, it had a great barbecue taste and was almost falling off the bones. The mothers had prepared potato salad, baked beans with strips of bacon across the top, a green salad with all the trimmings, and several cakes and pies for dessert. They all sat with two six-foot tables and chairs to seat everyone comfortably. The adults sat at one end of the table, and they sat at the other end with Scottie's little sister, Stacy. The parents seemed to get along great and had similar things in common. Of course, the men discussed their love for golf. Mrs. Trudy, Scottie's mom, offered to start picking up Abigail from school since they lived close by, and she picked up her children anyway. “It just makes sense, and I honestly don't mind at all,” she implied. Mrs. Mia agreed and thanked her.

“If there is ever an emergency or something where she can't. Just call me and I will be happy to do it,” Mrs. Patsy volunteered.

“Thank you both so much,” Mrs. Mia gratefully accepted.

After dinner, they all enjoyed two games of croquet before sunset. After nightfall, they all gathered around the fire pit for some s’mores. Scottie became lost in a trance as he watched

Abigail talk with Miranda. It was nice watching the fire display a dance with colors of orange, red, and moments of blue flames. He was mesmerized by the way Abigail's face glowed flawlessly in the light of the fire. Her eyes sparkled with happiness. Abigail must have felt his gaze on her because her eyes met his, and she smiled. He broke his glare and looked back down at the flames. *Real smooth,* he thought. He took a sip from his drink to quench his now-parched throat.

"It is getting late. We need start preparing to leave," Mr. Johnson spoke.

"It is nine o'clock. Time flies when you're having fun," Mr. Arnold chuckled.

"Yes indeed," Mr. Harmon agreed.

Mrs. Mia stood and began to collect the trash. The others joined in. "I have got this," she stated with an assuring smile.

"Nonsense. We aren't going to leave this mess for you to clean up alone," Mrs. Johnson answered.

"That is right. I will bring the food inside, and the girls can start the dishes," Mrs. Harmon volunteered.

"You truly don't have to..." Mrs. Mia interjected.

"We insist," Mrs. Johnson interrupted.

"It's the least we can do since y'all opened your home to us," Mrs. Harmon said.

"And it gets done a lot quicker when there is a team," Mrs. Johnson added with a smile.

"Thank you both. I do appreciate it," Mrs. Mia said, placing the empty cups and plates in the trash. While the women finished cleaning, Scottie helped the others pick up the furniture and placed them in the shed.

"This is nice. Did you do this all by yourself?" Mr. Johnson asked.

"Yeah, I took my time and worked on it here and there," Mr. Arnold answered.

"You definitely have talent in carpentry," Mr. Harmon said. "I am thinking of doing some remodeling to our kitchen. I could use some extra hands and someone who knows what they are doing. Would you mind assisting me?"

"It isn't all that hard. I don't mind helping if you aren't worried about some flaws here and there." Mr. Arnold answered.

"Can't be any worse than the way it looks now," Mr. Harmon replied, laughing.

"Let me know when you are ready to start, and I will be there." Mr. Arnold added.

The guys stood and listened as he showed off his carpentry work. After the Johnson's left, everyone sat around the fire Mr. Arnold and Mr. Matthew chatted about their jobs and other hobbies. Mrs. Mia was drinking her sweet, iced tea listening to Mrs. Trudy discuss her plans for a large block garage sale for all families. Miranda, Scottie, and Abigail decided to go into the game room and escape all the grown-up talk as they made one last s'more to go.

They played a pool game of cutthroat and talked about doing a small weenie roast for Labor Day. During their second game, Mr. Matthew came in to tell Scottie it was time to go. He said goodbye to the girls and went out after his dad.

"Do you like Scottie?" Miranda asked.

"What? No way. He is a friend," Abigail claimed. "What would make you think that?"

"I just saw how you guys are with each other and was curious," Miranda commented.

"What do you mean?" Abigail inquired, not sure what she was talking about.

"You two just seem to flirt at times." Miranda continued.

"No way!" Abigail interrupted. "I can guarantee you nothing is going on between us."

"If you say so," Miranda shrugged.

"I do say so," she assured her.

"Okay, so what is next?" she asked.

"Hmm. You want to watch some movies?" Abigail suggested.

"Sounds great. Let's shower and put on our pajamas to get comfortable," she stated.

"Great idea. I smell like smoke," Abigail laughed. "You can go first if you would like."

"Sure," Miranda said as she grabbed her overnight bag, and then headed to the bathroom.

Abigail wondered what Miranda could have meant by the way she and Scottie acted toward one another. Had he shown interest, and she did not see it? *He is cute,* she thought to herself, but she would rather not admit anything. What if he didn't feel the same, it could cause friction between them, and she did not want that for sure. She shook her head to clear her thoughts. She picked out a few good movies for the night and popped some popcorn for them to snack.

They slept in on Sunday morning after staying up all night watching movies and talking. Miranda went to get dressed, while Abigail collected all their trash from the night before. Mrs. Mia called over the walkie-talkie, "Good Morning girls. Are y'all up and about?"

"Yes Ma'am," Abigail answered.

"I have to go to town for a few things. Would y'all like to come along?"

"Miranda is changing. I can ask her and let you know."

"Sounds great. Over and out."

Abigail laid the walkie-talkie back down on the counter. She grabbed her a bottle of orange juice and a blueberry muffin to munch on while waiting on Miranda. She couldn't get the question Miranda had asked her last night out of her mind, *do you like Scottie?* She thought back to the first moment they spoke and how he was so friendly. His dark brown eyes and sweet smile. He made her feel so welcome on her first day of school. *I guess I do like him, but if he doesn't feel the same then it will ruin our friendship. We could never act the same around each other again. I surely* don't *want that, so I would keeping my feelings about Scottie Harmon to myself.* She thought to herself with slight disappointment, knowing the deep secret could never come to light. She was so far off in her thoughts that she didn't notice Miranda was now in the room. "Are you daydreaming about Scottie?" Miranda said with a tease.

"No way!" Abigail answered as she shook herself back to reality. "My mom is running to town and was wondering if we wanted to go with her. We could pick some items for tomorrow's hot dog roast and maybe even find some good shopping deals," she stated as she turned to face Miranda.

"What kind of girl would I be to pass up shopping?" she teased.

Abigail picked up the two-way radio, "Mom, you there?"

"Yes." Mrs. Mia answered.

"We are coming with you. How soon do we need to leave?" Abigail asked.

"When y'all are ready just come meet me in the kitchen," Mrs. Mia answered.

"I will go get dressed! See you in a few minutes." Abigail replied.

"Over and out," Mrs. Mia replied. The girls giggled and shook their heads.

"I am going to get dressed and be right out," Abigail stated as she grabbed her clothes for the day.

"I am going to play a game of Just Dance while I wait," Miranda answered as she turned on the game box and the television.

When Abigail was ready, the girls left to go meet Mrs. Mia in the kitchen.

"We are ready when you are, Mom," Abigail said as she and Miranda took a seat on the island.

"Okay, I am just going over my list to make sure I have everything down, so I don't forget anything," she answered as she glanced over the list. "All right, it looks like I have everything. Do you need anything for tonight or tomorrow that I need to add?"

"We were wondering if we could have a weenie roast on Monday. It would just be Miranda, Scottie and I," Abigail asked.

"I don't see an issue with that. Let me see what we may need," Mrs. Mia said, opening the fridge. "We have a pack of hot dogs, but I will add two more to the list to make sure that there will be plenty." She opened the pantry and looked in, "and we will need hot dog buns as well," she continued. She shut the door and walked over to the island and penned in the needed items to the list.

"Okay, I think I have everything. I will grab my purse on the way to the car," she stated as she grabbed the list and pen.

They returned a few hours later with the items needed. They helped Mrs. Mia put up the groceries. Once they finished, they went back to the game room and put on their swimsuits. They spent the rest of the Sunday relaxing and enjoying the pool.

Monday morning, they started cleaning and put away the pull-out bed. They stocked the game room with snacks and drinks. Miranda vacuumed while Abigail cleaned and mopped the bathroom. Once they had the game room cleaned and stocked, they gathered all the dirty laundry in a basket and walked to the house to see if Mrs. Mia needed help with anything. "Good morning!" Abigail called to see where her mom may be in the house.

"In here!" Mrs. Mia called out from the laundry room. Miranda and Abigail walked in to meet her. Mrs. Mia was folding and hanging clothes.

"Do you need help with anything?" Abigail asked as she placed the basket on the floor in front of the washer.

"The washer is empty if you want to start your load." She answered. Abigail placed the sheets and blankets in the washer with the laundry detergent and started the wash. "I am surprised to see you two up and about so early this morning." she teased.

"I guess I am too anxious to sleep," Abigail said with a smile on her face.

"What are you so anxious about?" Mrs. Mia asked.

"She is excited to see Scottie." Miranda snickered.

"Oh really, is there something I should know," Mrs. Mia smiled.

"I am not. We are just friends" Abigail snared. "I am just excited about the get-together with my friends."

"If you say so," Miranda laughed.

Abigail rolled her eyes. Mrs. Mia placed the folded clothes in a basket and turned to the girls. "I am going to put these clothes away. I cannot think of anything in here that may need to be done. You can go outside and check with your dad to see if he needs any help if you want."

When they got outside, they met Mr. Arnold cleaning the grill. "Hello, Dad. Can we do anything to help you prepare for tonight?" Abigail inquired. He took a glance around the yard.

"I don't see anything that needs to be done," he stated. "What time would y'all like to start the weenie roast?"

"I was thinking about six o'clock, but Scottie will be here around noon to spend the day," she answered.

"I have everything prepared and ready to go. I did most of the work on Saturday. You girls can enjoy the rest of your day," he said.

"You want to go and lay out by the pool?" Miranda asked Abigail.

"Sure, we can just relax until he gets here," Abigail answered. The girls went and changed into their swimsuits and laid out by the pool.

The girls were floating around the pool soaking up some sun rays when a big splash soaked them and sent waves into the pool. As they wiped the water from their eyes, Scottie emerged from under the water. "Oh, hello I didn't see y'all there." He giggled as he ran his hands through his now-soaked hair to pull it from his eyes.

"You think you are so funny," Miranda snapped.

"That is cold Scottie," Abigail shrieked.

"Oh, it feels good to me." he giggled. "So, this is what y'all have been doing all day?"

"Pretty much," Miranda said as she laid her head back down on the pool mattress.

"Must be nice to have nothing to do all day," he joked, treading the water to stay afloat next to them. "I guess I will go and get me a lazy mat to float next to y'all." He threw his mat in the middle of the pool and leaped into the water. The girls squealed as cold water splashed on them once more. Scottie giggled as he swam over to get on his mat.

"You are asking for trouble." Abigail jested.

"Wait till he is least expecting it girl. Then we will get him." Miranda taunted.

"Yeah, yeah. I am not scared of you two." he mocked as he pulled himself onto his mat.

"You should be." Miranda snapped.

They all floated around the pool and talked for an hour or so. Abigail noticed that Scottie had forgotten all about the revenge that she and Miranda had promised to come. She made eye contact with Miranda and nodded toward Scottie. He was laid back with his eyes closed with no regard that the girls were about to get their revenge. Miranda slowly moved her mat to the opposite side of his, and before he knew what was happening the girls splashed him. He was so startled that he flipped his mat, and their mats too. The girls came up laughing.

"We got you!" Abigail squealed.

"I knew what y'all were doing," he said as he wiped the water from his eyes.

"Yeah, you tell yourself that, but I saw your face. It said it all." Miranda giggled.

"Oh really?" Scottie scorned.

He turned around and splashed Miranda and the splash war began. Scottie tried to swim close to dunk them, but the girls reached the latter and were out of the pool before he was close enough. He climbed out, and the chase was on. The girls were screaming and laughing so loud that the entire neighborhood could hear the commotion and the fun they were having. Scottie caught up to Miranda first and pushed her in. When he reached Abigail, she wasn't so easy to push in the pool. She tugged and darted from him making it tough to get her in. Then Scottie ran toward her, wrapped his arms around her and with all his might, he leaned into the pool and they both went in. After their laughter died down, they swam for a little while.

"Anyone else thirsty?" Abigail asked.

"I am!" Miranda answered.

"Let's go in and grab a soda and a snack," Abigail suggested as she was climbing out.

"Sounds good to me," Scottie stated as he swam to the shallow end of the pool. He headed over to the chair where he had his bag of clothes and towel. "I called the bathroom first!" he called out as he sprinted for the game room door. The girls were still drying off.

"Okay," Abigail answered.

"Just don't take forever. I would like to change as well." Miranda teased.

The girls wrapped their beach towels around them and walked to the game room.

"I saw that flirting between the two of you." Miranda hinted.

"Flirting? What are you talking about? We were only having a good time." Abigail refuted. "If anyone was flirting it was you two." She accused.

"Ha-ha. No way! We are just close friends" Miranda snickered.

"Well, we are only friends too." Abigail insisted.

“No way. Not the way you two look at each other. There is more than friendship there.” Miranda remarked.

“Miranda, I think you're making something out of nothing,” Abigail claimed. “We are just friends, nothing more.”

“If you say so, but just know that you can confide in me when you are ready to accept it,” Miranda said with a smirk as she opened the door for Abigail.

“Nothing to accept. We are just friends and that is that.” Abigail whispered as she walked past her. They could hear the shower water running.

“I am going to grab a snack and soda while we wait. He will be in there awhile. You want to play a game of Just Dance?” Abigail asked as she pulled a dry sundress over her wet bathing suit.

“Go ahead, change the subject, but my confession box is always open,” Miranda remarked as she turned on the television and Xbox.

“Oh my, you are never going to let this go, are you?” Abigail shook her head.

“Not until you acknowledge that I am right.” Miranda scoffed.

Abigail grabbed a soda and shut the door. “Well, I hate to break it to you, but there is nothing to acknowledge or confess.” she insisted as she popped the soda open. Miranda walked over to the refrigerator and grabbed a drink. “Yeah okay.” She giggled as she opened her soda. Abigail laughed and shook her head as she walked over and grabbed a remote to start the game. Scottie came out as they were finishing their third dance.

“I call seconds!” Abigail squealed as they ended the song. Once they finished, she grabbed her bag to head to the bathroom and turned around so fast that she and Scottie bumped into each other. Their eyes met as they were standing face to face. He smiled down at her with his curly strands dangling underneath his ball cap. Abigail was startled and jumped, “I am so sorry,” she apologized as she moved a lock of hair from her face.

“No worries,” he answered. She rushed off into the bathroom to keep him from seeing her blush.

“Yeah, just friends” Miranda uttered under her breath with a smile.

Abigail leaned with her back on the door as she locked it with her hand behind her. She eased her breathing as her heart was beating out of her chest. *Oh my! He is so cute!* She hung her bag on the hook that was on the back of the door. She unzipped it, took out her change of clothes and started the shower.

“You like her, don’t you?” Miranda questioned Scottie when she heard the shower cut on.

“Who, Abigail?” Scottie asked as he opened his soda.

“Yes! Who else would I be referring to?” Miranda stated.

“I am not her type.” Scottie insisted.

“Her type?” Miranda snickered.

“Yeah,” Scottie said as he grabbed a bag of chips and sat down at the bar. “She is pretty, smart, funny, and has a great personality. Why are you asking me this? Has she said she likes me?”

“No. I just saw y’all flirting with each other and was curious.” Miranda explained. “So, you do like her?”

“Yes, but like I said she is out of my league.” He declared.

“I knew it!” Miranda yelped.

“Well, I would like it if you didn’t say anything. If she doesn’t like me, it will make it awkward, and I don’t want that.” He asked.

“Your secret is safe with me,” she smiled.

“Thank you. Now let’s play a game of nine ball.” He gestured as he rose and walked toward the pool table. They had finished their game of nine ball and were playing a game on the XBOX when Abigail exited the bathroom.

"It's about time!" Miranda shrieked. "I am freezing in these wet clothes." She jumped up, grabbed her bag, and sprinted for the bathroom. As Abigail went to sit down, Mrs. Mia called out over the handheld radio "Hey kiddos! Are y'all in there?"

"Yes, Ma'am," Abigail answered.

"I am heading to work," she stated.

"Yes ma'am. Be safe and have a good night," Abigail said.

They enjoyed the rest of the day playing games, swimming, and roasting hot dogs and s'mores.

*The Boy is Mine – Brandy & Monica*

# CHAPTER 5

## Summer Splash

Abigail checked her reflection in the mirror. Her bikini halter top and gray shorts complemented her tanned skin. She pulled her hair back in a ponytail. Her nerves were getting the best of her. She squeezed her hands to stop them from shaking. Everyone was arriving for the summer splash to celebrate the end of their summer break.

"Scottie is bringing Amy," Miranda called out from behind the closed bathroom door. She is on the cheer squad." Abigail looked over Amy Harold in her mind as if she was standing right in front of her. *Blonde hair, blue eyes, and a perfect tan, with a fresh manicure and pedicure, and high maintenance attitude*. "How can I compete with that? Oh, what do I care? Deep breaths," she mumbled to herself. She sat down on the edge of her bed and closed her eyes. She inhaled deeply through her nose and exhaled the air slowly through her mouth. Hoping to calm her racing heart.

"Are you okay?" Isabella asked as she came into the room.

Abigail jumped from being startled. "Oh, yes. I am fine."

"Then why are you so jumpy if you are fine?" She continued.

"I was just lost in my thoughts, and you caught me by surprise." Abigail snapped in.

"Are you upset because Rhett couldn't make it?" Isabelle asked.

"Of course not." She stood and began to put away the clothes that were strewn all over her bed.

"Of course, why would you be with Scottie here every day? He is so handsome. Are you sure you have no feelings whatsoever for him?" Isabella pressed on.

"Shh. Someone may hear you," Abigail peaked out into the hallway to make sure no one was there and shut her door.

"You act as if it is a secret that you have a crush on Scottie. I am almost positive that everyone knows, so why act like it is a huge secret?" Isabella continued.

"I agree!" Miranda shouted.

"You need to tell him and get it over with. I think you have known him long enough, and from the way Miranda talks, he likes you too."

"I am almost certain he does," Miranda cut in.

"He has a girlfriend you know?" Abigail interrupted.

"That is only because you kept pulling his chain, and so he probably just decided to move on." Miranda snapped in.

"Pulling his chain?" Abigail asked.

"Don't act so innocent. You know you flirt with him and then deny any feelings for him." Miranda added.

"We are just friends, and haven't you watched Dawson's Creek. Didn't you see how it continuously ruined Dawson and Joey's friendship? Why would I do such a thing to our friendship?" Abigail explained.

"Yes, and I am assuming that Rhett would be Pacey in this situation. Well, except Rhett and Scottie aren't best of friends." Isabella said.

"We will never be more than friends no matter if there are feelings or not. I would rather have him as my best friend rather than no relationship." Abigail said.

"Oh. So, you do have feelings for him?" Miranda nudged.

Mrs. Mia opened the door. "What are you girls shouting about in here?"

"I was just telling Abigail that she needed to..." Isabella stated.

"She was just telling me to relax and not be so nervous," Abigail interrupted, giving Isabella the keep quiet look.

"Yeah, she is all jittery and shaking. I was telling her she needed to calm down." Isabella played along.

"Are you ok?" Mrs. Mia asked.

"Yeah, I will be fine. It is just the first time all my friends will be together, and I just hope everything goes smoothly." Abigail answered.

"Girls, you need to come down and join the party," Mr. Arnold called from the bottom of the stairway.

"On our way," Abigail answered. They came bouncing down the stairs and out the back door. A lot of people started to arrive and there was so much going on, from swimming in the pool to water balloon fights.

"Hey, let's get two teams together and play some volleyball," Miranda stated. Mr. Arnold had built the court with sand for Abigail and Miranda's team to play and practice.

"I like the sound of that," Abigail agreed.

"If anyone is interested in playing volleyball, then meet us by the net," Miranda screamed over the music and laughter. Some of their teammates joined in as well as Isabella and Scottie. Miranda and Abigail were chosen to be captains. They took turns picking their players until both teams were complete. They enjoyed playing that before they knew it two hours had went by.

"I am going to cool off in the pool," Beth called out as Abigail's team scored the winning point.

"Me too," LaTonya called out as she ran to catch up with Beth.

"I do need something to drink," Isabella said.

"Wait up," Miranda shouted. "I am coming too." She skipped up next to Isabella. "So, are you having fun?"

"Lots. I hate that I must leave to go home tomorrow. These few weeks have flown by way too fast." She replied.

"Well, you know what they say. Time flies when you're having fun." Miranda stated. Isabella nodded in agreement and grabbed a bottle of water from the ice chest. "Look at the two of them. You cannot tell me there are no sparks between them." She tilted her head toward Scottie and Abigail, still standing by the net. Abigail was standing with her arms behind her back as she leaned against the pole. Scottie was holding onto the net with his left hand letting it hold his body weight as he leaned into it. His shirt sleeve fit tight over his flexed biceps.

"I don't think we are the only ones noticing," Isabella nudged toward Amy who was making her way over to them.

"Let's go get our girl," Miranda said. They jogged over. "Abigail, what you say we go get our tan on. We are losing daylight."

"Sure," Abigail answered. "Talk to you later Scottie." He nodded as Amy was still giving him the third degree about leaving her by herself with strangers.

"She really is a piece of work," Isabella stated as they applied their suntan lotion on.

"You have no idea," Abigail chuckled. The sun was beginning to set, and some were having a water balloon fight. Chad tossed a ball at Mark, but he missed, and it burst by Abigail's chair. The cold water splashed on her and she leaped up with a squeal.

"I am so sorry Abigail. I meant to hit Mark and missed," he apologized.

"Yeah, sure you were," she teased.

"Honest," he said, drawing a cross over his heart.

Mark tossed a ball at Miranda, and she gasped for air. The cold water took her by surprise.

"You are going to pay for that," she shouted. She ran for the bucket of water balloons, and the water fights began. They were all running around, hiding and attacking one another. Josh, who came with a neighbor down the street, joined the fight. He drew his arm back and hit Abigail right in the gut. The balloon busted and soaked her as if he had thrown a bucket of water on her.

"You just messed up, boy. It's on now!" Abigail squealed. She grabbed two water balloons, and the chase was on. Josh tried hiding behind a bush, but as he was coming down the other side of the stairs Abigail spotted him. She reared back with her pitching arm and let it fly.

It struck Josh right in the chest, and without any warning, Abigail felt a sharp pain in her right cheek with a loud slapping noise. Josh disappeared just as fast as his handprint appeared on her face. She stood with her hand on her face. Scottie heard the loud hit and stood up looking around to see where the noise came from. His gaze landed on Abigail standing with a shocked look on her face. She was holding her hand to her cheek. Amy saw the fire in his eyes. She stood and grabbed him by the arm, but he broke from her grip. He was at Abigail's side as quick as the Flash. "Abigail are you okay?" he asked as he pulled her hand away from her face. A perfect handprint was bright red across her cheek. "Abby, who did this? What happened?" He asked as he began looking around for the culprit.

"It's okay," she stated while trying to gather herself.

"No! It's not okay! Who did this?"

By now everyone stopped what they had been doing and focused on the commotion. "I think his name was James or Josh. He came with one of our neighbors," she said. Abigail began to feel awkward with how everyone was focused on her.

By this time Amy was at Scottie's side, "Scottie, you need to calm down. You're making a scene." She grabbed his arm trying to cool his nerves.

"I won't calm down! Where is he? What does he look like?" Scottie started scanning the crowd for him and swung his arm back out of Amy's grasp.

"What is going on?" Miranda asked as she and Isabella arrived to see what the commotion was all about.

"A coward slapped Abby," Scottie hissed.

"What? Who?" Isabella looked around to see who could do such a thing.

"Guys, honestly, it is nothing," Abigail insisted.

Mr. and Mrs. Whittinger heard what had just taken place and came out to check on Abigail. "Abigail, are you okay?" Mr. Arnold asked, turning her toward him with both hands on her shoulders.

Mrs. Mia saw the mark on her face as the light hit her cheek. "Oh my! Abigail, who did this?" She pulled her hair back to try to get a better view of her face.

"One of the boys that came with the Smiths from down the street," Abigail murmured as she folded her arms wishing everyone would stop making it bigger than it was. He hit her and she just wanted to go back to the way things were before the incident.

Her Dad turned and was storming off, "I'm going to have a conversation with him right now!" Mr. Arnold, with Scottie hot on his trail.

"Mom, can we please go inside?" Abigail whispered, nudging her head toward the house.

"Of course," Mrs. Mia comforted her. As they turned to go inside, Mrs. Mia looked at the crowd that was gathered and murmuring among one another. "I think the party is over now. I am sorry for having to end it so soon, but please gather your items and head home," she apologetically asked them, and then she and the girls went inside the kitchen. Mrs. Mia grabbed an ice pack that is for emergencies out of the freezer, "here sweetie, this should help with the swelling" she suggested, "what happened out there?"

Miranda, Isabella, and Amy sat down next to Abigail at the bar. "We were just having fun with the water balloons. He threw one at me and soaked me, so I in turn chased him down and threw one at him. It hit him in the chest and the next thing I knew he started walking up to me. I was laughing because it was just playing around you know, but he slapped me. Mom, I still don't know what I did wrong," Abigail stammered with tears flowing down her cheeks.

"You did nothing wrong, Abby!" Scottie bellowed as he and Arnold came rustling through the door. The girls turned to face them. Abigail wiped the tears from her face.

"He is right. The only one in the wrong is that boy, Josh," Mr. Arnold agreed as he re-examined her face now that they were in a better light.

"He better pray there isn't any bruising or else he will have tougher consequences than just a good talking to." Scottie huffed as he took a seat at the end of the bar.

"We made it very clear that he is not allowed here nor to have any kind of contact with Abigail," Mr. Arnold assured as he prepared a pot of coffee. "I believe we have put the fear of God in him, Scottie. I am sure we won't have to worry about him messing with her ever again," he chuckled as he started the coffee pot.

"No disrespect Mr. Arnold, but he better count his lucky stars that you and Mr. Smith were there to help me control my anger, because I was about to rearrange his face," Scottie scoffed as he clenched his fist tightly.

"Now there is no need in you getting your feathers all ruffled over this Scottie. Mr. and Mrs. Whittinger have this all under control," Amy snapped while giving him a harsh look, and if looks could kill they would be planning a funeral.

Mr. Arnold and Mrs. Mia looked at one another with a look of, *oh no, someone isn't so happy*. Amy isn't the first girl they have seen get jealous of Abigail.

"Well, honestly, I don't think everyone needed to overreact the way they did. I am a big girl, and I can handle myself," Abigail snorted, and placed the ice pack on the island.

"No boy has the right to put his hands on you!" Scottie snapped back. He glanced at Abigail while shaking his wrinkled forehead and waving his hand in the air in gesture.

"Again, boy's hands on Abigail are none of your business," Amy smarted off in her snotty, rude voice.

"I think it's time for us to go," Scottie sighed, as he hopped off the stool. Miranda and Isabella were holding in their laughter from Amy's outburst.

"I will walk y'all out to the car," Abigail said as she got up from the bar following them out the door.

"I don't think someone is going to last much longer." Miranda giggled once they exited the room. The others snickered.

Scottie stopped in front of the car while Amy jumped in the driver's seat and started the car.

"I am sorry she is so mad," Abigail stood with her arms crossed, trying to warm up her body from the cold, damp clothes.

"Don't mind her. She is just upset because she wasn't the center of attention tonight."

"Thank you for taking up for me," she said as she pulled a loose strand that escaped from her messy bun from her face.

"No need to thank me. I always have and I always will," he assured her as he placed his hands in his pockets.

Abigail blushed, "but you know I can take care of myself. I am starting to cause issues with you and Amy," Abigail urged, hoping that he would see she wasn't a little girl anymore.

"Look I am not apologizing for protecting you. I am sorry, however, for making you feel uneasy and awkward. I know you hate having everyone focus on you. As far as she goes," glancing back at Amy, who was sitting in the car on the phone with most likely Mari Kate, her best friend, complaining once more how Abigail ruined another night for her. Scottie continued, "Well she can get over it or move on either way, won't hurt me." He looked back at Abigail. "No worries, no frets, okay, bestie?" He reassured her as he lightly slugged her in the arm.

She smiled back "Okay."

He hugged her goodnight, and she waved to them until they were out of sight.

Abigail went back into the house. Mrs. Mia and Mr. Arnold had joined Miranda and Isabella at the bar talking and drinking coffee.

"Well, the handprint is nearly gone," Mrs. Mia gestured to Abigail's cheek as she leaned on the bar next to her.

"See no need for all the fuss and ruining a perfect evening," she stated as she wiped her hand across the granite as if she was wiping it clean.

"Scottie is right. No boy should ever hit you. A boy has no right to hit a girl no matter the situation. Josh needed to be confronted to know that what he did would not be tolerated here," he rebuked as he sat his coffee cup down on the bar. "How is Amy doing by the way?" he gushed, giving Mrs. Mia a look.

"She is upset. I tried to apologize to Scottie, but he told me not to worry about Amy," she sighed.

"I bet he did," Mr. Arnold giggled and took the last sip of his coffee.

"Okay, that is enough funny jokes," Mrs. Mia snickered.

"I don't like being the thorn in their relationship. I try to be her friend, but she just doesn't like me," Abigail lamented.

"Well, everyone knows that you and Scottie have grown closer since we moved here a few months ago. He is very protective of you like a big brother, and I for one am thankful. It puts me at ease knowing you're in good hands when he is around," he explains, "but no girl in his life will ever be happy if they can't come to the acceptance of your friendship." He got up from the bar and set his empty coffee cup in the dishwasher. "What about some s'mores and a night of stargazing?" He inquired as he looked out the window to the backyard. "It would be a waste of good firewood if we put it out now," he suggested as he turned to them, raising his eyebrows.

"I am down for that," Miranda stated.

"Me too," Isabella agreed.

"That sounds good to me. Just let me run upstairs to change into something cozy and get out of these damp clothes," Abigail agreed as she tugged at the now-damp tee shirt. The girls ran upstairs for Abigail to change.

While Abigail was picking out comfortable, baggy clothes to change into, her phone started ringing. She looked over at it on her bed. AMY CALLING. *What? Amy? Why is she calling?* "Hello," she curiously answered.

"We need to talk," Amy ordered.

"What does she want?" Miranda whispered.

"Okay," Abigail said in a questioning tone as if to say I don't understand. Shrugging her shoulders to Miranda and mouthing I don't know.

"I am getting tired of this babe-in-distress thing you have going on." Amy stated.

"Babe-in-distress?" Abigail chuckled, "I have no idea what you are talking about." Isabella and Miranda looked curious to one another. "Babe-in-distress?" Isabella whispered. Miranda motioned that Amy was crazy by twirling her finger in a circular motion at her temple.

"Yes, and don't act all innocent like you have no idea what I am talking about." She continued,

"Amy, I am sorry for what happened tonight. Everyone overreacted and ended a perfectly good party." Abigail relented in a sincere voice, trying to calm Amy down.

"You don't have to apologize to her!" Miranda shouted.

"Hang up the phone!" Isabella insisted.

"It's not just tonight. Every time you are in trouble you come to my boyfriend like he is your knight and shining armor who comes to your rescue, and it needs to stop!" Amy yelled.

"What?" Abigail gasped as if someone knocked the air out of her lungs. "I don't! Look Amy I didn't like the outcome as much as you obviously, but your issues of jealousy are out of my control, so I am not sure what you are expecting."

"Hang up the phone," Miranda and Isabella whispered.

"YOU LEAVE SCOTTIE ALONE!" Amy interrupted in an outraged roar, "THAT IS WHAT I EXPECT YOU TO DO!"

"Well, Amy, Scottie and I are best friends and nothing more. You keep making things out of nothing. I won't stop being his friend just because you think you have control over me. You need to grow up and stop acting like a spoiled brat!" Abigail shuttered out of shock, covering her mouth. Shocked at the words that just escaped her mouth. *Whoa, what was that? Where did that come from?* Hello," Abigail whispered to see if she was still on the line. Abigail looked at the phone, "Huh, she hung up," she shrugged. "That felt good to get off my chest, but I could have done it a different way. Oh well," Abigail murmured as she laid the phone back down.

"You go, girl! It's about time you stood up to her," Miranda squealed.

"I didn't see that ending coming," giggled Isabella.

"Neither did I. It just came out," Abigail said.

"What did she say to that?" Isabella asked.

"She hung up," Abigail answered.

"That was so great to watch! I am so proud of you. Maybe she will learn to stop being so petty and stop acting like a first grader," Miranda stated.

"Yeah, right," Abigail giggled.

"Go get changed. We have some s'mores waiting for us downstairs," Isabella insisted.

"Oh, yeah. I forgot what I was doing in all the commotion," Abigail laughed. She grabbed her change of clothes and went to the bathroom.

"Man, this has been one crazy night!" Isabella said.

"That is for sure," Miranda agreed.

*More than Friends – Jason Mraz (feat. Meghan Trainer)*

# CHAPTER 6

## Sophomore Year: 2012-13

Freshmen year flew by way too fast. Scottie, Miranda, and Abigail became inseparable. They spent so much time together that others started calling them the three musketeers, because if you saw one, then the other two were not far behind. They were all known as close friends, but everyone knew that Scottie and Abigail's friendship was a lot closer. They started their high school years at Windsor Forest High School, Knights. Scottie was picked on the football team as the quarterback, and Abigail was on the softball and volleyball team. She was also on the Student Council and in the yearbook club.

It was 4th period in Mrs. Harris's Algebra class. Peter Thornburg and Abigail were messing around with each other before class. Abigail gave Peter a little shove after one of his corny jokes, and as Peter came back with a harmless shove of his own, Scottie walked into the classroom. Not aware of the horse playing that was taking place between the two. He moved and shoved the desk out of his way until he reached Peter. Scottie pushed him with all his might. The confrontation was on. Abigail tried to explain that it was a playful shove, but Scottie wasn't listening. "Keep your hands off her," his face was blood red.

"Sorry, man. We were just goofing off," Peter through his hands up in the air as if he was surrendering.

Abigail ran out into the hall. Tears started streaming down her red face. She was so embarrassed and upset that Scottie reacted in such a way.

Scottie met her in the hall. "Did he hurt you? Are you okay?"

Abigail answered in her angry tone, "No! Why did you do that, Scottie?"

"He was pushing you around," he replied as he looked back at Peter in the classroom, who was sitting at his desk probably trying to figure out what he did wrong.

"You know I am not going to tolerate someone bullying or hurting you, Abby." He sneered as he leaned against the wall with his hands and glanced over at her.

"Scottie, Peter and I were messing around. I pushed him first," Abigail explained, calming down when she saw how concerned Scottie was.

"When I walked in and saw him push you … I, I just lost it," now he pressed against the wall so hard, his knuckles were turning white, "joking or not joking, no boy has the right to put his hands on you like that Abby," Scottie murmured as he pushed himself off the wall. He looked at her, "no one should, and if I am ever around when they do, then they will answer to me." He said softly. He walked past her and entered the classroom.

Abigail went to the bathroom to throw cool water on her face to help with the redness and take the heat out of her face. She grabbed a brown napkin from the dispenser and dabbed her face dry.

"*What was he thinking? Why would he act in such a way? I have never seen Scottie get physical with anyone. Say a few choice words or confront someone, yes, but not go to the extreme of* *getting physica*l," she asked herself in puzzle. Just then, Miranda dashed into the bathroom.

"Are you okay?" She leaned on the sink next to her.

"Yes, I am fine. Puzzled, embarrassed, but I am fine." She answered as she tossed the balled-up napkin in the trash.

"What happened? I saw you crying, and Scottie didn't look too happy either." Miranda inquired.

"Honestly I am still trying to figure it all out myself," Abigail answered. Just then, the door swung open "There y'all are. The bell is about to ring, and you will be tardy." Mari-Kate stated, holding the door open.

"Oh my, I didn't realize I was in here that long," Abigail stated as they exited the bathroom and headed to class.

"We can talk more later," Miranda suggested as they reached the classroom just as the tardy bell rang.

When Abigail was seated in her seat, Scottie tapped her, "are you okay?"

"Yes," she answered sharply. He leaned back taking the hint that she was still mad at him.

Mrs. Harris took her place at the front of her class. "Please turn to page ten in your textbook." Abigail still was a little upset at his reaction. She looked over at Peter and waited for him to look her way. After a few minutes with no luck in getting his attention, she opened her book and class began.

After class, she hurried to catch up to Peter before he went away. "Peter," she called out before he could leave the room and mixed in the crowded hallway. He turned to face her with his red auburn hair and green eyes. His face had light freckles across the base of his nose. They always made Abigail think of angel kisses, at least that is what her mom called them. "I am sorry for how Scottie reacted," she implied as she reached him.

"Well, I don't see where it is your place to apologize, but the truth is I am still trying to figure out what I did for such a reaction out of him. We have been friends since kindergarten, and he has never approached me like that," he answered as he ran his hands through his hair.

"I am just as puzzled as you are. In the hallway, he was asking if I was okay and if you had hurt me?" She said as she brought her books to her chest with her arms crossed over them.

"Hurt you? I would never do such a thing. I was just messing around. I am truly sorry if I did," he said with a concerned tone.

"NO! You didn't hurt me. I knew we were just teasing each other. I just don't see why he was thinking such a thing," she interrupted.

Peter started laughing, "Oh, I see where his reaction is coming from. He only saw part of what was happening… the part where I pushed you. I know why he acted that way. I should have seen it, but not until just now."

"Well please enlighten me!" she insisted.

"Scottie is very protective of you." He said, looking at her as if she should have known already what caused the whole thing to happen.

"I get that he is protective, but I have never seen him react in such a physical way before, and that doesn't make it right for him to confront you like that." She exclaimed.

"Well, I know how he is about you, and I should have known better than to be horseplaying with you like that." He implied.

"'How he is about me?' We are just friends, Peter. Nothing more." She snapped.

"You may be just friends, but Scottie protects you like a lion protects his lioness." He exaggerated with a smile. "Rest assured no one in their right mind would hurt you with Scottie around, and I should have known better myself. Remember how he acted at the summer splash when that boy slapped you? I knew better than to horseplay with you."

"It was just horse playing and you did nothing wrong, I will need to talk with Scottie later to get this all under control before this happens again," she sneered. "We better get to the next period. I will see you tomorrow."

"Have fun with that," he whispered as he walked away.

Abigail stayed in thought the rest of the day on Peter's words of Scottie protecting her like a lioness. *We are just friends. Is this how all guys see Scottie and I? Are they too scared to ask me out in fear of what Scottie may do or say? Why is he so protective over me? He and Miranda have known each other longer than I... why is he not protective over her in the same manner? Is there more that I am not seeing, or more that I* don't *know? Ugh, what I am thinking? That is crazy! Scottie just sees me as a little sister, nothing more and nothing less. I am sure if that was Stacy, he would have reacted the same way. Yeah, see that is all it is. I am just a sister to him. That explains it.* She nodded to herself and turned her attention back to Coach Cox, who was teaching the latitude and longitude of the maps, pointing at the diagram he had projected on the screen.

The final bell rang. She walked down the hallway and met up with Miranda on the way to her locker.

"So, what is up with you and Scottie?" Miranda questioned.

"Well, if you listen to how Peter explained it, one would think we had a thing for one another," Abigail answered.

"Well, it doesn't take a scientist to see that." Miranda cut in.

"What are you talking about? Don't start this again! He only sees me as his little sister, and that is it. We are nothing more!" Abigail yelled.

"If you say so." Miranda added.

"I know so, and you know I am not his type anyway. He likes the popular, pretty, California blonde girls. He would never look at me in that way."

"Girl, you need to open your eyes and see he has it bad for you and so do you for him. Everyone else sees it. You two are just too stubborn to admit it." Miranda remarked, "But maybe one day y'all will come around."

They arrived at Abigail's locker, she opened it, placed her books from the last period in it, and pulled out her backpack.

"Whatever! You are crazy to think such a thing." Abigail giggled as she started placing her supplies for homework in her bag.

"What is she thinking up now?" Scottie inquired as he walked up beside them to his locker. "Well actually..." Miranda started to speak.

"Nothing but girl conversation that you wouldn't be interested in hearing." Abigail interrupted and gave Miranda a look as if to say 'don't say another word'.

"Well, I best be on my way before I miss my ride. Talk to y'all later." Miranda called as she turned and walked away.

"Speaking of rides, we better get going before your mom leaves us. We must get in line to pick up Stacy at Hesse." Abigail closed her locker, tossed her backpack on her shoulder, and started walking toward the exit for the car riders.

Scottie slammed his locker, "I will never understand these two." He whispered to himself.

"Hello there, I was beginning to think you two were lost or something." Mrs. Trudy said when Abigail opened the door to get in the back seat.

"No ma'am, we were just running a little behind," Scottie said as he climbed into the front seat. "Did y'all have a good day?" Mrs. Trudy asked as she pulled out of the school.

"Yes ma'am," Abigail smiled at her in the rearview mirror. There was only a slight conversation between them on the way to pick up Stacy. Abigail was so lost in thought over what Miranda and Peter had said to her that she barely even conversed with everyone. Stacy slid into her seat, "hey!" she smiled as she closed the door.

"Hello," Abigail returned with a smile.

"I am tired!" she said as she laid her head back against the headrest of her seat.

"Was it that bad of a day?" Mrs. Trudy asked.

"No ma'am. Just long," she exclaimed. "You won't believe what happened in P.E. today," she said as she sat up straight in her seat with excitement. "We were playing volleyball, and I was in the front row in the middle, and the ball was being hit back and forth," she gasped. "It was hit towards me. I jumped and spiked it on Heather Markwell," she laughed out loud. "I couldn't believe it happened, but her reaction made it even better. She was so shocked that she stomped and screamed in anger. Man, it felt so good and honestly it may never happen again. It was just one of those once-in-a-lifetime moments that will be etched in my memory forever. I mean she is an actual volleyball player, and I am not so can you imagine it." Stacy laughed continuously. "I guess you just had to be there. It was awesome!"

"Good for you!" Abigail stated with a smile.

They all started up a conversation. Abigail looked at Scottie as he was laughing and cutting up with Stacy. She drifted off in thought… '*could he have feelings for me that I am not seeing? Is it true?'* She looked at him, his skin was tanned from being outside in the sun playing sports.

His eyes filled with joy as he joked and teased his little sister. His smile could brighten up her darkest of days. '*Uh! What am I doing? This is Scottie! The one who only dates cheerleaders and popular girls! My best friend!*' she shook herself and looked out of her window.

Scottie noticed as she turned her head away. *She hasn't said anything since we have been in the car. Much less since we got out of school, she must still be upset with me.*

"Scottie? Hey, earth to Scottie!" Stacy snapped, pulling his attention back to her.

"Huh, Oh I am sorry Sis. What did you say?" he asked as he turned and looked back at her.

"I was wondering if you would want to watch a movie or something together after dinner?"

"Sure, that will be great!" Scottie answered.

They pulled into Abigail's driveway. "Bye Abigail" they called out as she slid out of the car. "Bye," she smiled and shut the door. Mrs. Trudy put her vehicle in reverse.

“Mom, do you mind if I stay for a bit with Abby? I wanted to discuss some of my homework with her that I am not sure how to do.” Scottie said as he grabbed his backpack.

“Sure, but be home before supper.” Mrs. Trudy stated.

“Yes ma’am,” he replied as he opened and shut the door. He called out to Abigail. “Hey Abby, wait up!” She turned in surprise seeing Scottie sprinting toward her. “I can tell you are still upset with me from what happened with Peter.”

“Peter explained that he understood why you reacted that way,” Abigail said as she placed her bag on a bench by the front door.

“WHAT?! What did he tell you?” He asked cautiously.

“That you were just protecting me, and that he should have known better than to play in that manner with me. Especially when you were around.” She explained.

“Well, I’m glad he got that through his head, but that is all he said?” He continued.

“Yes, why? What else is there to say?” Abigail asked, waiting to see if there was more she needed to know.

“No, of course not. He knows you are like my little sister and that I am protective of you, so he should have known how I was going to react.” Scottie said as he sat down on the rocking chair.

“I do appreciate you looking out for me, but next time can you not go all hulk on someone before you know if I am hurt or not?” Abigail asked with a smile.

He laughed out loud with his head thrown back, “I will do my best, and if you say it was just horse playing, then I will call and apologize to him later.”

"But if I am ever in trouble, I am glad I have you in my corner," she said with a smile. She sat down on the bench beside her backpack.

Scottie looked over at her and moved a loose strand of hair from her face, "I always have, and I always will."

*You're the One I Want – John Travolta & Olivia Newton John (Grease Soundtrack)*

# CHAPTER 7

## Sock Hop

Their sophomore year was going great! Scottie was the quarterback, and the football team was playing 3-0. Abigail and Miranda were picked to play on the volleyball and softball teams. The first few months had flown by, and football season had already started. It was now mid-October and the holidays were coming up fast. Abigail woke up and laid out her clothes for school and went to take her morning shower. Once she was dressed, the aroma of someone cooking filled the air. She put on her shoes and took one last look in the mirror. *Looks good to me and* ran downstairs to the kitchen.

"Good morning, Mom," Abigail called out as she came into the kitchen.

"Good morning, sunshine!" She answered as she placed the last pancake on the plate. "Did you sleep well?" she asked as she sat the plate down in front of Abigail on the island.

"Yes ma'am." She replied as she smothered her pancakes with syrup.

"Would you like some pancakes with your syrup?" Mrs. Mia giggled as she poured herself a cup of coffee.

Abigail looked up and smiled, nodding her head yes. "What better way to eat them?"

Mrs. Mia winked, "You have enjoyed them that way since you were little. What is on the agenda today?" She inquired as she sat down on the stool next to Abigail.

"Well, I don't have any tests, thankfully! Unless someone decides to throw a pop quiz at us, which I seriously hope not since I didn't bring any books home for the weekend. I haven't studied any of my notes from last week's work."

Mrs. Mia sat her cup down after a sip of her coffee, "I am sure if anyone could pass the pop quiz it would be you."

"I am so glad you have faith in me because I sure don't," Abigail murmured as she cut another bite of her pancakes.

"I know you are capable of much more than you give yourself credit for." Mrs. Mia added.

"We are working on a school dance that will be coming up next month before we let out for the holidays. We are leaning more toward having a 1950s theme with poodle skirts and all." She said before taking a bite.

"Wow! That sounds amazing!" Mrs. Mia exclaimed.

"It has been so much fun getting everything together. I was wondering if you would have time to make me a poodle skirt." Abigail asked as she washed down her pancakes with orange juice.

"Sure. How soon will you need it?" Mrs. Mia asked.

"Hmm, let's see, the dance is scheduled for Saturday, November 11th, so I think the week before would be okay. If you have time? If not, that is okay. I am sure we could buy one." Abigail stated.

"That is a little over a month away. I am sure that will give me ample time to make it for you." Mrs. Mia assured her as she placed her empty cup in the dishwasher.

Abigail got up from the stool and grabbed her plate. "Thank you! I know it will look awesome!" she gushed as she rinsed the plate off in the sink and placed it in the dishwasher.

"You are welcome. Are you ready to go?" Mrs. Mia asked as she grabbed Abigail's lunch bag from the fridge and placed it by her backpack. “Let me go brush my teeth and I am ready.” She called out as she ran up the stairs.

The car ride was nice with the sun shining. Abigail and Mrs. Mia discussed the ideas for the dance. When they arrived at the school, Abigail hugged her mom and stepped out of the car. “I love you. Have a good day,” Mrs. Mia called out as Abigail placed her backpack on her shoulder.

“I love you, too. Be careful going home.” Abigail replied and closed the door. She turned and walked into the school.

“Hey there,” Scottie called out as he walked toward her.

“Good morning.” Abigail answered.

“Are you ready for another day in this dump?” he asked as he opened his locker.

“It isn’t that bad Scottie.” She grabbed her 1st-period books from the locker.

“Hey!” Miranda said as she reached her locker.

“Hello there,” Abigail answered.

“Morning,” Scottie mumbled.

“What’s wrong, Scottie?” Miranda inquired.

“You know he is not a morning person, so he is still a little grumpy for having to get up early and be here one more day,” Abigail teased.

Scottie nudged her, “you know me so well.”

“I sure do,” she smirked.

“No better than I do,” Amy snorted as she came up behind Scottie, giving Abigail the evil eye.

“Hello, Amy,” Abigail said with a smile.

Amy just rolled her eyes and slid in between her and Scottie. “Are you ready to go to the first period, Abigail?” Miranda asked in a not-so-nice tone, aggravated at Amy’s attitude as she slammed her locker shut.

“Yeap.” Abigail answered as she shut her locker door. “See you later, Scottie,” Abigail called out as they walked away.

"She gets on my last nerve!" Miranda snapped, as they walked down the hall to the classroom.

"She doesn't like me," Abigail said, shrugging her shoulders.

"Huh, she better watch how she treats you in front of Scottie, or she will be his ex-girlfriend very quickly," Miranda informed her. "She should know that by now, at least one would think," she said, rolling her eyes.

"Scottie likes her a lot, so I don't see her being his ex any time soon. We need to get along with her for Scottie's sake."

"NO, I DO NOT!" Miranda shouted so loud that everyone in the hallway stopped and looked at them.

"Girls, you don't have to shout over everyone. Remember to use your inside voice while in the school building. No screaming or shouting is allowed, or you will have lunch detention." Mrs. Harris reminded them as they passed her door.

"Yes ma'am," they answered in sync. Abigail elbowed Miranda "Keep it down, will ya?"

Miranda giggled, "Sorry, not sorry. I don't have to be nice to her. If Scottie chooses to be associated with that self-involved, haughty girl, then that is his choice. I don't have to put up with her, nor do I have to pretend to be her friend."

"I am just saying that we should be the bigger person here and not stoop to her level," Abigail suggested. "Whatever girl. I will catch up to you after class," Miranda said as she turned to go to her 1st period.

"Ta Ta," Abigail waved as she walked to her class.

The first three periods flew by quickly. Thankfully as she had hoped so far, there were no pop quizzes. *Great it's lunchtime* Abigail rubbed her belly which had been rumbling for the last hour. She placed her books in her locker and grabbed her lunch bag. "Hey, you do remember that our committee is meeting today at lunch, right?" Mari-Kate asked as she was walking up to Abigail's locker.

"Yes, I was grabbing my lunch bag and headed there." Abigail answered.

"We can walk together," Mari-Kate suggested.

"Let's go," Abigail answered.

The girls walked to the round table under the tree, where the committee had their meetings every other Monday. Miranda, Deidra, and Sara were already seated eating their lunch while waiting. "Hey guys," Sara greeted them as they took their seats.

They each returned the hello. Mari-Kate and Abigail began eating their meal and listened to the other girls discuss the decoration and announcement ideas. An hour later, the girls had all their plans laid out and were ready to begin finalizing everything. "It will be here before we know it, so don't procrastinate on your part. Here is the list of your duties one more time. Sara, you are to oversee the decorations. Abigail, call the DJ that was suggested by Deidra's mom to discuss availability and prices. Call around to check prices and availability of some photographers who can take the photos. Mari-Kate, get a list together of snacks and drinks. Also, ask around to see if some parents and teachers can volunteer. Deidra, gather some examples of the flyers and posters that you have in mind. We will all discuss our ideas, pros, and cons at our next meeting." Miranda stated.

"We are on it," Sara assured her. The bell rang and the girls gathered their items and threw away their trash. "Abigail, when are you going to go shopping for your poodle skirt?" Miranda asked. "Oh, I forgot to tell you that I already talked with my mom, and she is going to make mine," Abigail replied.

"Oh, wow! Do you think she could make me one as well if my mom purchased the material and other things?" Miranda questioned.

"I am sure she won't mind, but let me check with her and then I can let you know," Abigail answered.

The weeks flew by just as Miranda had warned the girls it would, but everything went smoothly with only a few hiccups.

They started the decorations on Wednesday and finished Friday evening in time for the game. The Knights won the game by a field goal 20-17, what a way to end the season! Miranda and Abigail had planned for a sleepover at the Whittinger's home. Mrs. Mia picked up pizza on the way home.

It was a little after eleven o'clock PM when they pulled into the drive. "Girls, can you grab your pizza?" Mrs. Mia asked as she turned off the car.

"Yes ma'am," Abigail answered as she came around to the passenger door to grab the pizza off the seat.

"I have stocked the snack cabinet and fridge with drinks for y'all." Mrs. Mia stated as she met them at the trunk.

"You spoil us, Mrs. Mia," Miranda joked.

"I just like to make sure y'all have everything you would need, so you wouldn't have to go back and forth from the house. Less likely for dirt to be tracked in the house, which means less cleaning for me to do," she teased as she closed the trunk.

"Ah, now I see the real reason. And all this time I thought it was for us," Abigail said with a sarcastic jester.

They all laughed. "You guys have a good night. Don't stay up too late." Mrs. Mia said as they entered the laundry room.

"Yes ma'am," Abigail replied. Mrs. Mia hung her purse on the rack by the door and went upstairs.

"I am worn out. What do you say to just a movie tonight? After a hot shower of course," Miranda suggested.

"Sounds great to me," Abigail agreed as she opened the back door.

The girls walked down the walkway that Mr. Arnold installed a few days before with a string of solar lights. "I like this walkway. It is way better than trying to carry a flashlight with your hands full." Miranda commented.

"Yes indeed," Abigail answered as they reached the door to the game room. The girls showered and ate their pizza while they watched *A Walk to Remember*.

"I could watch that movie a million times and never get tired of it," Miranda stated as the closing credits displayed on the screen.

"I know what you mean. I just hope the man I fall for will love me like Landon loves Jamie." She collected the trash to throw away.

"You already have someone that loves you that way," Miranda snickered.

"What? Who are you talking about?" Abigail asked with a puzzled look.

"Why do you act as if you don't know what everyone else knows," Miranda cut in.

"I truly don't know what or who you are talking about," Abigail defended.

"Then you are truly blind not to see Scottie is in love with you." She fluffed her pillow.

"WHAT?! He is not! He is in love with Amy! You know his girlfriend." Abigail snorted.

"Oh my, you are blind." Miranda added.

"We are just friends and nothing more," Abigail stated as she climbed in on her side of the sofa bed.

"You keep telling yourself that," Miranda murmured as she turned off the lamp on the end table and climbed into the sofa bed.

"Speaking of Amy. I hope she is okay after her horrible accident in the cheer squad tonight. I wonder if she will make it tomorrow night." Abigail inquired.

"Changing the subject, I see." Miranda said.

"Yes and no. I am seriously concerned for her well-being." Abigail added.

"We can call her tomorrow if you are so worried about her." Miranda said.

"I just might do that." Abigail continued.

"I would love to see how that call will go, that's if you even get an answer." Miranda stated.

"Yeah, you are right. I just don't know what to do to get her to like me." Abigail agreed.

"She knows exactly what I know and what you don't want to admit." Miranda continued.

"Okay, on that note I am going to sleep." Abigail dismissed.

"Hmm, hmm. In denial and blind. Not a good combination," Miranda snickered.

"Hush and go to sleep," Abigail murmured as she jokingly kicked Miranda's leg. The girls giggled. A few minutes later, silence fell over the room as they both drifted off to sleep.

Abigail woke up to the sound of the birds singing. She looked at the clock on the wall, it was 10:15 AM. She stretched for a few seconds before getting up. She went to the bathroom and got dressed for the busy day ahead of them. "Good morning," Miranda called out as she got out of bed.

"Good morning. I am almost done," Abigail answered.

"What time is our appointment at the salon for our hair and nails?" Miranda asked as she started folding the bedding.

"I believe Mom scheduled it for noon so that we would not be in a rush."

"Okay, that sounds good. I just didn't know if we were in a rush or not." She grabbed her overnight bag and headed to the bathroom when Abigail came out.

"No rush." Abigail assured.

"I will be out in a few," Miranda said as she closed the door. Abigail called her mom on the intercom to let her know that they were up and about.

"We need to leave here within an hour," Mrs. Mia reminded her.

"Yes ma'am," Abigail answered. Abigail went to the cabinet and pulled out a box of fruity pebbles and made herself a bowl of cereal.

"Are you getting some fruity pebbles?" Miranda called out.

"Yes." Abigail answered.

"Would you mind making me a bowl too? I am almost finished." Miranda stated.

"Sure," Abigail said and pulled out an extra bowl from the cabinet.

The girls finished the cereal and cleaned up their mess from the night before. It was 10:45AM as they folded the bed back into the sofa.

"Let's call Scottie and check on Amy." Abigail suggested.

"You are still worrying about her?" Miranda snapped in.

"She may have been seriously injured and I am just concerned that is all. I mean she couldn't even walk and had to be carried off the field." Abigail continued.

"You know as well as I that she would not be concerned if it was you that was hurt," Miranda stated as she grabbed her night bag as they started out the door.

"You may be right, but we have to be better than her." Abigail advised.

"You amaze me, Abigail Whittinger." Miranda shook her head.

"Why? What do you mean?" Abigail inquired.

"No matter how she treats you, you still are nice to her. You and I aren't alike, because I want to give her a good slap across the face. Which would have happened if not for you holding me back." Miranda snorted.

"I just don't want to stoop to her level, and I hold you back for her sake." Abigail stated.

Miranda's head flung back as she laughed at Abigail's statement. "If she knew what was good for her, she would stop pushing my buttons because one day she is going to go too far."

Abigail laughed and held the back door for Miranda to enter. "Mom, do I have enough time to call Scottie?"

"Sure. Is everything okay?" Mrs. Mia asked.

"Yes ma'am. I just want to check on Amy to make sure she is okay from the cheer mishap last night." Abigail explained.

"Yes, that was very scary," Mrs. Mia said as she wiped down the island.

Abigail picked up the phone and dialed Scottie's number. It rang a few times and then it went to voicemail. "Huh, no answer. Guess we will see them at the dance," Abigail said as she hung up the phone. "Ready when you are, Mom."

They had a blast at the salon joking around with one another, and the hours went by quickly. They went back home to get dressed. "You girls are so beautiful with your curly ponytails and bows. Your skirts bring me back to the good ole days." Mr. Arnold commented on them as they came down the stairs.

"Thank you!" Abigail answered as she gave her pink poodle skirt twirl at the bottom of the steps.

"Thank you for making my skirt, Mrs. Mia," Miranda said.

"You are welcome. Does it fit okay? It twirls great with the slip under it," she giggled, referring to Abigail's skirt twirling.

"Yes, ma'am it does," Miranda answered.

"Mom, we need to be at the school no later than 4:30 PM so that we can all be there when the entertainment and refreshments start arriving," Abigail stated as she looked at the clock, "Oh my, it is 4:00 already! Will you be able to take us now?"

"Sure, but I want to take a few pictures of y'all in front of the fireplace before we leave," she stated as she grabbed her camera off the sofa table.

The girls grabbed their hands and skipped to the fireplace. They posed for what felt like 20 pictures. "Okay, Hun. I think you have plenty of them," Mr. Arnold teased.

"Yeah, Mom this isn't prom," Abigail said sarcastically.

"Okay," Mrs. Mia said as she placed the camera back on the sofa table. "I will have double prints for both of you to have one each," she said as she turned to head out the door.

"That sounds great," Miranda answered.

They arrived at the school right on time. The rest of the crew was already there. Deidra was directing the parents who volunteered with the food and other items to their tables. Mari-Kate was at the refreshment table placing everything in its designated spot as it arrived. Sara was at the DJ table, which was decorated like a huge jukebox, assisting the DJ with getting everything set up.

Everything looked amazing! The floor was covered with pink, red, white, and black balloons. A huge balloon arch ended in a huge decoration that was designed like a shake for the backdrop for photos. Also, a red 1955 convertible Ford Thunderbird, which was loaned by a parent, was parked next to it as well, to be used for photos. It was a classic show car and was in mint condition.

"Can I help with anything?" Miranda asked Deidra as she came to the entrance.

"If you can assist with making sure everything is brought to the proper place so that we don't get backed up as the volunteers bring in their items," Deidra answered.

"Of course. I can take the ones who are here to volunteer with the dance, and if you would like you can assist with the ones bringing the food," Miranda suggested.

"That works for me. We can divide them up into two lines," Deidra agreed. Deidra was dressed in a red skirt with a white poodle dog, a white top and black knit sweater that she left unbuttoned, and a red scarf tied around her neck. It complimented her dark complexion very well. She had on a pair of white Keds and black, ruffled folded ankle socks. Her hair was pulled back in a short ponytail with a white bow.

"May I please have all volunteers that are here to chaperone and serve to form a line in front of me," Miranda shouted loud enough that the crowd could hear her. Of course, it wasn't hard to know which were there to assist, because they were all dressed for the theme. It was as if she stepped into the movie Grease. Men with their leather jackets, white t-shirts, slick back hair, folded-up jeans, and tennis shoes. Women with their vintage dresses and hairstyles, or their poodle skirts and sweaters. It was just magnificent how it was all coming together, and everyone dressed in the occasion of the 50s theme.

Abigail went inside to make sure everything was set up and ready to go when the photographer arrived. Once she had everything in place, she walked over to the DJ booth. “Can I assist in any way?” She asked.

Sara had a black skirt with a pink poodle dog, a black button-down shirt with the sleeves rolled up three-fourths of her arm, a pink bandana wrapped around her curly black hair-like headband, black socks folded at the ankle, and a pair of white tennis shoes. “I believe we have him all set up,” Sara answered as she looked around the booth.

“It looks so good, Sara. You did an amazing job with the decorations,” Abigail said as she gazed around the gym.

“Hey, it was a team effort, remember? I didn’t do this all alone,” Sara reminded her.

“Yes, but these are your ideas. We just helped to put them all together,” Abigail stated.

Mari-Kate, Deidra, and Miranda met them at the booth once they were finished. “Wow! This looks good guys,” Miranda said as she also took in all the decorations.

“We make a good team!” Mari-Kate answered.

“I agree,” Deidra said.

The DJ started playing the music at 6:30 PM for the earlier arrivals. The chaperones and servers were in their positions as everyone started drifting in. At first, everyone was scattered about at the tables that were set out for seating while they ate. No one was volunteering to be the first on the dance floor.

“What is with no one dancing?” Scottie questioned.

“I guess no one wants to put themselves out there to look like an idiot,” Abigail said as she turned to face him.

"Well let's give them something to talk about. What do you think?" Scottie asked, holding his hand out for her.

"Me? Why not Amy? Was she able to make it?" she asked, looking around for her.

"No, she tore her ACL and was ordered on bed rest and lots of icing by her mom until they see the Orthopedic doctor next week," he explained as he nudged her with his hand that was still out waiting for her to grasp.

"Oh boy, you are asking for trouble aren't you," she teased as she grabbed his hand.

"Come on Abby don't you remember? Trouble is my middle name," he jested with a devious smile. He had his brown wavy hair slicked back, with gel, a black leather jacket with a white t-shirt, jeans with the hem rolled up at the ankle with white tennis shoes. *He sure wears this style well,* Abigail thought. A chill went all over, and she shivered slightly. Scotty saw her shake a little, "Are you cold," he asked.

"No, just a chill ran over me," She answered.

"That tends to happen when a girl touches my hand," he teased.

"Ha, you are very funny," Abigail said with a laugh. "Where are we going? I thought you wanted to show them how to get the party started?" Abigail asked in confusion when she realized they were not headed for the dance floor.

"I have a few things up my sleeve," he joked. They arrived at the DJ booth. "Hey, do you have 'The Twist' or 'Twist and Shout'?" Scottie asked.

"Sure man. I can play that," the DJ stated as he started looking for it in his song list.

"Oh, you are good," Abigail said flirtatiously.

"As I said, I have a few things up my sleeve," he winked.

'Twist' started blaring over the speakers as they joined hands and strolled out on the dance floor. He gave her a little twirl and they started doing the twist. Miranda and the girls ran out to join them with the others not far behind. They all laughed, giggled and enjoyed dancing to the song. When the song ended, Scottie and Abigail went to the refreshment table to grab some punch to quench their thirst. "I am sorry Amy isn't here to enjoy this night with you. How is she doing?" Abigail asked as she filled her cup with some punch.

"I hope this doesn't sound bad, but I am kind of glad she didn't come," Scottie stated as he grabbed a glass.

"Why? Is everything okay?" Abigail asked.

"Yes. I just can be more laid back, and not be so uptight. When she is around, I really cannot be myself." Scottie answered.

"What do you mean?" She moved toward the snacks to see if any looked appetizing to her.

"Well, for instance, the fun we just had on the dance floor would not have happened if she was here." He downed his punch. "She would have made a big deal out of it for sure."

"But we were just having fun," she said.

"Yes, but she gets a little crazy whenever you are involved. She is so jealous." Scottie shook his head.

"Jealous? Of me?" Abigail turned with a look of shock on her face. "She has no reason to be jealous of me." Scottie shrugged his shoulders and tilted his head as he munched on a cookie.

Miranda came to the table. "Hey! Are y'all going to stand around and talk all night?"

"We were just catching our breath," Abigail said.

"I guess that is our queue," Scottie said as he finished another glass of punch and tossed it in the trash. "I am going to go catch up with my teammates. I will dance with y'all a little later." He turned and walked toward the table where a few of the football players were seated. "So, what was all that about?" Miranda asked.

"What are you talking about?" Abigail said with a questioning look.

“Fine, I can see you aren’t going to share, so come on let’s have fun before we have to leave,” Miranda stated as she grabbed Abigail’s hand and pulled her to the dance floor.

Scottie sat at the table talking with his friends, when he heard Abigail’s giggle carry over the music. He looked over at her and the girls dancing. *She is crazy not to see why Amy is so jealous of her. She is beautiful. She lights up any room she walks in.* He got lost in his thoughts watching her. “Earth to Scottie,” Patrick called out. Patrick was the offensive tackle for the team. He is 5’9, with black hair in a military cut style. His eyes are hazel, and they are shining green tonight. He also had his hair slicked back with gel. They all matched in their black leather jackets, white t-shirts, ankle-rolled jeans, and white or black shoes.

Scottie jumped and turned, “What? Oh, sorry. I got lost in thought.”

“I can tell. You were way out there,” he teased. “We were asking if you had heard from Amy.”

“Oh, yeah. She is fine. Just watching TV with ice on her knee and her leg propped up. She was texting me so much that I put my phone on silent, so I would not be disturbed by her anymore. I am here to have fun. Not to stay on my phone fighting with her all night.” He answered as he turned in his chair to face them.

“I don’t see how you deal with all of that. She has to constantly watch you and be pampered. She probably has one of her friends spying on you right now.” He said as he gazed around the room.

“She has her moments, but she isn’t that bad,” Scottie snickered.

“I agree with him.” Miranda pulled out a chair to sit at the table. “I tell Abigail the same thing.”

“Y’all make her out to be worse than she is,” Abigail spoke up, taking a seat across from Scottie.

“I agree,” Scottie said.

"All I am saying is I think you deserve better," Patrick stated.

"Yeah, like Abigail," Miranda suggested.

"WHAT?" Abigail screeched as her cheeks became very warm, and a hint of red started to appear on them.

Scottie looked at her. *Wait, does she have feelings for me that I am not aware of? Miranda is her best friend. Why would she say something like that?*

"We are just friends. He is like a big brother that I never had. Why does everyone assume that our friendship is anything more than that," Abigail assured her. Scottie looked down at the table hoping she didn't see the way he was looking at her. *I knew it was too good to be true.* "Right Scottie?" Abigail asked. Scottie lifted his head, "Yes that is right. We are nothing more than friends, and you guys need to stop attacking Amy. Yes, she has her faults, but no one is perfect either."

'You broke my heart because I couldn't dance. You didn't even want me around, but now 'I'm back,' came blaring over the speakers as the song Do You Love Me by The Contours started to play over the speakers. Scottie, Miranda, and Abigail jumped to their feet with excitement. "Let's boogie!" Abigail squealed with excitement. Scottie, Abigail, Patrick, and Miranda ran to the dance floor. They split up into couples. Abigail and Scottie started dancing and singing loud to the music. "How do they not see it?" Miranda shouted, nodding toward Scottie and Abigail.

"I honestly don't know. It is kind of transparent if you ask me," Patrick replied.

"I agree 100%, but if you ask them, they both deny it," Miranda said. "Maybe one day they will see what we have seen all along." They both giggled and continued dancing.

It was beginning to get close to the end of the night, and they decided to take group and couple photos. Scottie and Abigail took a photo together in the red convertible. She scooted beside him on the bench seat. His hand rested around her on the seat. *Oh my, he even smells good*, she thought as his cologne filled the air around her. Miranda and Abigail climbed on the back of the Thunderbird to sit down. They placed their feet in the back seat and looped their arms with one another. All the photos turned out so good that everyone purchased a copy of them for each to take home. It was a night to remember for years to come.

*One Call Away – Charlie Puth*

# CHAPTER 8

## County Fair: 2013

Junior year is here. *Where has the time gone? It seems like I just moved to Savannah yesterday, and now I only have two years left of school,* Abigail thought as she sat in $2^{nd}$ period. It was October and the county fair was in town. Some of them would be going together for a date night. Abigail had no intention of going. She normally liked to wait until Sunday when she could purchase the bracelet and ride an unlimited number of times. She returned her attention to Coach Jones who was teaching their history lesson, which was her favorite class.

Xavier is Scottie's friend, and he also plays center, the one that hikes the ball to the quarterback, on the football team. They have played football together since he joined the team last year. He is a little shorter than the other guys, around 5'6. He is of medium build. He and Scottie were close but not as close as Scottie and Abigail, of course. Xavier has a nice olive complexion that tans very well. With eyes that blend into certain colors when he wore them. A dirty blonde hair that he lets grow out in the winter, but he normally had the fade cut with the top just long enough to pull off "The Mizz" spike. He is very laid back and easy to joke with. Loves making everyone laugh, which is why he was voted the class clown for the last two years and will most likely be elected again this year.

He wanted to ask Abigail to go with him to the county fair. It's not like it will be an actual date or anything because every guy knows she is all about her books, and sports, but then she is a fun person to hang out with. He pulled the date night tickets from his pocket to make sure they were still where had he put them. The bell was about to ring for lunch, and that will be the perfect time to ask her.

They were all at lunch and sitting at their usual round table. Scottie and Amy were sitting next to one another, sharing carrot sticks. Amy brings her lunch if you call rabbit food lunch. Scottie nibbled on items he could manage to scuff down. Sometimes she would bring a bag of chips and soda for him, to use as a bribe to get something she wants. Abigail was sitting at the table reading her book and crunching on a bag of Gardetto's Rye chips. Xavier went and slid in next to her.

"Hello bookworm," he joked, "What are you reading there?"

"Maze Runner Death Cure by James Dashner." She explained as she showed him the black and blue cover of the hardback book. "My parents and I are going to rent it after I finish reading the book. I like to read a book before the movie just to be able to see how different the movie is from the book."

He looked at the book, "I guess that is cool if you are into reading. I don't have the patience for it. I would prefer the movie over a book any day," he replied. "Hey, while I have your attention I wanted to ask. Are you doing anything tonight?"

Abigail looked at him awkwardly, "Hmm. I don't think so. Why, what's up?" she inquired.

He pulled the tickets from his pocket. "Well, a few of us are going to date night at the fair. I was wondering if you would like to go only as friends of course," he suggested while holding up the two tickets. "I figured why not take advantage of the 'date night' where two rides for one," he implied while rubbing the tickets together between his fingers.

"Sure, why not. I love going to the fair," she responded with a smile, "I am sure it will be fun."

"Great. It's a date then. No, I mean. . ." he started to explain.

"I know what you mean Xavier. It will be fun," she interrupted, rescuing him from stuttering even more.

"A date?" Amy asked as if shocked that Xavier asked Abigail out.

"No, I have over-spoken. I asked Abigail to be my riding partner tonight at the fair," Xavier corrected Amy before anyone gets any bright ideas or wrong impressions.

"That is cool, we will be there as well," Scottie stated as he squeezed Amy with his arm around her.

"I believe that Mari-Kate and Ricky are going as well," Amy responded.

"Going where?" Avey asked as he and Miranda joined them at the table. Avey is the wide receiver for the football team. He is 5 '10, muscular, and has light brown skin. His black hair is curly, but he keeps it cut close to the skin on the sides with the top long enough for the curls to show. With big brown eyes and long eyelashes. All he has to do to get his way is to give you those sweet puppy eyes, bat those beautiful long eyelashes, and you will give in quickly. He is quiet at first, but he opens up once he gets to know you. He has a great personality, gets along with almost everyone he meets, and is very smart. He takes his football seriously but not to where that is his only concern. He and Miranda have been dating since the summer splash.

"To the fair tonight. I just asked Abigail to be my partner for the rides tonight," Xavier said as he nudged Abigail with his elbow, and smiled.

"Oh, we are going too! Wait, you two are going on a date?" Miranda inquired, seeking for more information.

"No, it isn't a date. We are, how did you put it, Xavier," she evoked as she tilted her head toward him. "Oh yeah, taking advantage of two riders being able to ride for the same as one."

"Okay, if you say so," Miranda teased as she smirked at her. They all giggled.

"It's going to be fun with us all there. What time are you planning to meet?" Scottie asked.

"Well, I would like to eat before we get there," Avey suggested before taking a bite of his BBQ beef sandwich.

"Yes, we know," Miranda giggled, "Food is always first on your agenda for anything."

"Hey, us guys have to eat," he teased.

"Okay, how does 7:00 PM sound?" Xavier asked.

"That is good for me, we eat dinner at 6:00, and I can be ready and there by 7:00," Abigail stated as she marked her page with a bookmark, closed her book, and placed it in her backpack.

"Everyone agrees?" Scottie questioned as if taking a vote. Everyone nodded in agreement. "So, 7:00 it is."

The weather was perfect for a night at the fair. A soft breeze blew in the night air. It carried all the wonderful scents of the fair straight to your nostrils that made your mouth water with the smell of popcorn, funnel cakes, and candy apples all at once. The lights from the rides filled the sky with just enough light to see where you are walking. You could hear the music from the Himalayan ride as you entered the front gate. The screams and laughter from the rides filled the air with excitement.

After the boys purchased the tickets, they were on their way. Their stomachs were turning flips with mixed emotions from being joyful to fearful. Trying to calm their nerves and mustering the courage to ride those rides, you know the ones that the boys were going to dare the girls to ride, like the zipper, and the spinning alien ship.

As they were walking by the games, the concessionaire started to taunt the boys about knocking down a stack of cans to get their girl the gigantic stuffed animal. The one that he ends up carrying the rest of the night. He was smart because he knew that you don't mess with a boy's ego in front of girls. As they walked closer, they could see there were ten rows of cans stacked in fives.

"Okay, you have my attention. What's the objective of this one?" Scottie answered the taunting of the concessionaire. Intrigued by the looks of the game.

"Alright. It's not that hard. You get five balls for $5.00. Whoever knocks over the stack of cans gets the animal of choice for their girl," he explained and pointed at the stuffed animals hanging above.

"Well, that sounds easy to me! Normally I throw to moving targets, so this should be a walk in the park," Scottie boasted while reaching for his wallet in his back pocket.

Scottie wore a straight-leg, relaxed pair of Levi jeans, a yellow long-sleeve shirt with the word Columbia written down the left arm in navy, his yellow Converse shoes, and a white baseball cap.

"Why don't we make it a game for all, boys versus girls, and the team that wins gets their choice of animal?" He coaxed all of them as he lifted the bucket of softballs.

Abigail strolled up next to Scottie and elbowed him in the side, "How about it, slugger? You think you have what it takes to beat us girls?" she mocked. She was dressed in a pair of Maurice blue jeans, a rose-pink sweater with the Savannah written in dark gray across the chest, and white K-Swiss sneakers. Her hair was pulled back in a messy bun with a few loose new hairs around her face.

"We sure do!" Xavier interrupted as he started pulling a ten-dollar bill from his wallet. "I will pay for us both," he said as he gave the concessionaire the money and pointed at Abigail. Xavier wore a slim-fit American Eagle jeans, with a charcoal Hollister t-shirt, underneath an unbuttoned checkered long-sleeve shirt with the sleeves rolled up to his elbow, and black Nike Air Max Torch 4 sneakers. All the boys followed, paying for their dates as well. Now the concessionaire was pleased, knowing he did his job very well to get the entire group involved in the game.

"Show me that arm you have on you," Mari-Kate cheered on her date, Ricky. Mari-Kate is Amy's best friend. She is also on the cheer squad but is nothing like Amy. She is much sweeter, and that makes her an easy pushover for Amy to boss around. She had her hair pulled back in a ponytail with a white ribbon. She had on her red cheer hoodie with "WARRIORS" written on the front in white, with a pair of khaki shorts, and white and black Vans.

"I will do my best," he snickered as he winked at Mari Kate. Ricky is the running back for the football team. He's 5'9, 250lbs of pure muscle, with red, wavy hair. He has light freckles on his cheeks that go across the ridge of his nose and match his brown eyes. Though he may look like a bully, you will find he is just a big teddy bear with a big heart once you get to know him. He is always looking out for others, making sure that they are staying hydrated, and safe, and not overdoing it in the weight room. He wore a Cinch jeans light washed jeans, a tan Mossy Oak t-shirt, boots, and a camo Under Armor cap to keep his red hair out of his eyes. He walked up to pay the concessionaire and the guy glanced back at the girls and back to Ricky.

"My money is on this big guy," he egged on the competition as he collected the money from Ricky.

"Don't count your chickens just yet," Abigail declared with a hand on her hip.

"Move over boys, let me show you how it's done," Xavier bragged as he pushed his way between Avey and Scottie.

The boys had their five balls stacked in front of them, and they started their game by picking up the first one and tossing it. Scottie missed the target, realizing this was not as easy as it looked. Behind him, he heard Abigail snicker. He glanced over his shoulder as if to say that now is not the time.

"Now you see what it is like to throw at a real target," she teased, still giggling. Amy rolled her eyes and looked at Mari-Kate.

"Here we go," she mumbled under her breath. Mari-Kate just shook her head and hoped that this wasn't another one of those nights.

Xavier, Ricky, and Avey knocked off the top can with their first toss. Scottie knocked off the first can with his second toss. Avey and Xavier cheered, "Yeah!" as they knocked over their last cans. Leaving Ricky and Scottie with knocking down their remaining cans. Ricky and Scottie had knocked off the next two with two remaining and with only one more ball left. Xavier and Avey were cheering them on, "YOU GOT THIS," they cheered. While the girls were teasing them for not being able to knock down all their cans. Ricky reared back with all his might, threw the ball and missed. Then Scottie picked up his last ball, taking time to get a good look at his target, brought his arm back as if going for a touchdown, and then tossed the ball, but it missed. Leaving them with two cans remaining.

"Alright girls, step up and show these boys how it is done," the concessionaire called as he stacked the girls' balls in fives on the counter. Miranda took her place at the counter and picked up her ball, tossing it back and forth in her hands.

"Abigail has this in the bag. We are going to smoke these boys," she joked. Miranda wore a peachy pink long-sleeve shirt with a Salty Vibes surfboard logo on the back in teal, which she bought in Pensacola during their summer trip, with relaxed fit Levi jeans. Her curly hair pulled back with a light blue jean baseball cap and multi-tropic Vans. She pulled her sleeve up to her elbows as if it was about to get serious. Amy rolled her eyes and picked up her first ball. She chunked it with all her strength but missed. Amy wore a dark wash, boot cut jeans, a grey top with black and white plaid sleeves, a rose gold sequin pocket on the left side, and a pair of black and white plaid slip-on round-toe flat sneakers.

"Whoa, what a throw you have there, Amy," Abigail complimented out of shock, "You should try out for our softball team. We can use you at shortstop."

"No thanks," Amy sneered.

"Suit yourself," Abigail replied, shrugging her shoulders as she picked up her first ball to throw, but also missed.

"Not so easy to hit that still target after all, aye, Abby?" Scottie chuckled with his right leg out to put his weight on, and his left hand in his pocket. Abigail just glared and nodded as if to say watch this. "Come on Amy! You can do this!" Scottie cheered.

Amy picked up another ball and chunked it, knocking off the top can. She tilted her head at Abigail with a smirk thinking, *beat that.*

Miranda and Mari-Kate were able to knock down three cans with their first two balls. "Looks like Mari-Kate and Miranda should teach you two how it's done," Avey pestered.

Abigail hurled her second ball as if aiming at the catcher's glove and knocked only the top can off. "Something is wrong, I know I hit that harder, and on target. All the cans should have fallen," Abigail fussed.

The boys snickered behind her. "Maybe it's not the game, but the pitcher itself," Amy hissed.

"That's enough, Amy!" Miranda declared.

"Calm down, girls," Xavier said, moving his hands in a downward motion as if trying to lower the girl's rising hormones.

"It's alright, it's all for fun," Abigail reassured Miranda.

"Speak for yourself," Amy said sharply as she threw her third ball, missing the target again.

Just then Mari-Kate shrieked with joy, "I DID IT!" As she knocked over the last few cans with her last ball.

"How did you do that?" Miranda asked, shocked that hers were still standing as well.

"It's easy, just aim and throw. Just throw it as if you're throwing one of those softballs to get a player out," Mari-Kate instructed her.

Miranda reared back with her last ball, and BAM! Her last two cans fell. "YES!" she squealed and leaped into the air. She and Mari-Kate gave each other a high-five.

"Come on girls! We're in your corner!' Miranda cheered on Abigail and Amy.

The guys all exchanged glances, "We may be having a tiebreaker," Ricky jabbed.

"Not having that," Abigail sharply stated, shaking her head.

"Come on, Amy! Put all you got into it!" Mari-Kate encouraged.

Now it was down to the two of them, and Amy wasn't just playing around. She wanted to knock her cans down before Abigail. Amy mustered up all her anger and picked up her last ball. Abigail's main concern was beating the boys. She drew back her last ball. Not realizing it, both girls released their balls simultaneously. BOOM! All the cans came crashing down. "YAY!" Mari-Kate, Miranda, and Abigail all cheered while giving each other high-fives.

"What's wrong?" Mari-Kate asked Amy. "We won! You should be excited," Mari-Kate persisted.

"Yippee," Amy sarcastically stated while twirling her finger in the air. She did not share the same enthusiasm as the other girls. She was not too happy that she didn't beat Miss Goody-Two-Shoes, Abigail. Amy wanted to show her up.

"Alright," Abigail hopped over to the concessionaire. "What do the winners get?"

"I keep my word, each of you girls gets to choose their enormous stuffed animal," he explained, pointing to the prizes above them.

"I don't want one of those ugly animals," Amy hissed.

"Well, I want the pink gorilla," Abigail stated while pointing to her choice.

Scottie put his arm around Amy, "Are you sure you don't want one?"

"No," she mumbled.

"My choice is the tiger," Miranda said with a big smile.

"I'll take the teddy bear! It reminds me of Ricky," Mari-Kate explained, winking at him.

"Hey, don't ruin my image," Ricky chortled.

"Thanks for a great time," Xavier thanked the concessionaire as they all walked away.

They walked over to the concession stand to grab some snacks and drinks. Ricky ordered a caramel apple for himself, a waffle cake, and two drinks for himself and Mari-Kate. Avey ordered some kettle chips on a stick and loaded it down with ketchup, a waffle cake, and two drinks for himself and Miranda. Scottie ordered a foot-long corn dog with lots of mustard for himself, a bag of popcorn for Amy, and two drinks. Xavier ordered nachos with lots of cheese and peppers, a waffle cake with extra powdered sugar for Abigail, and two drinks. After getting all their food and drinks, they started walking, looking, and deciding which ride they would ride first. Xavier wanted to ride the zipper, which no one was jumping at the bits to ride.

"Who would want to ride that after eating all the food we are eating? We all know it will just come back up after being spun around like a twirling top toy?" Miranda answered.

"Let's try a few calm rides to give the ladies' foods time to digest, and then move on to the more fun rides," Avey joked. He wore a white Adidas cap that was trimmed in black. His curls were coming out from under the bill. He had on a gray hoodie with the logo and Adidas in black on the front, with black Adidas joggers. A pair of black X-LPR Adidas sneakers.

"Okay, so what would they like to ride first on the carousel?" Ricky laughed.

"No! I don't want to ride kiddie rides, I just don't want to lose the delicious waffle cake I just had," Miranda explained.

"Well, how about the Ferris wheel?" Scottie asked as he pointed to the big, bright, and tall wheel that was lit up with lights, which were changing colors as it turned.

"I am up for that!" Abigail said as she finished the last bite of her waffle cake. Licking the powder off her fingers.

"Yes, that I can handle," Miranda agreed.

"Are we all in?" Xavier questioned as he looked at everyone. "Ferris wheel is our first ride?"

Everyone nodded in agreement, and they got in line. All the guys pulled out their tickets to board the big wheel. You could feel the nice breeze from it as it turned. It was slowing down to start letting the passengers off one by one. As others got off, it would move to the entrance to allow passengers waiting to board. It sat up to four people in each cart. Their cart arrived, and Scottie, Amy, Xavier, and Abigail boarded- with Scottie and Amy on the left and Xavier and Abigail on the right.

"We'll meet you guys back down here at the exit afterward," Abigail called to those waiting to board the next cart.

"Have fun!" Miranda said waving bye at them.

"Now don't you boys get any ideas about rocking this thing back and forth," Mari-Kate said as their empty cart stopped for them to board.

Ricky and Avey just smirked at each other. "Why would we be so childish to do such a thing like that to you when we all know how scared of heights you are," Ricky snickered. They all boarded the cart with Ricky and Mari-Kate on the left, with Avey and Miranda sitting on the right. The ride went up and would stop every few minutes, letting others board until every cart but two were occupied. Then it started turning at a nice, steady speed. It was a nice night to ride because it wasn't hot or cold. It was 75 degrees, and with the turning of the wheel, it gave a nice breeze.

"I think this was a great choice for a first ride tonight," Scottie stated as he put his arm around Amy.

"It is nice," she said with a grin.

"I love looking at the city at night with all the lights shining," Abigail commented as she looked down at the city below them lit up with lights in the night sky. "It is so beautiful."

"Yes, it is beautiful," Scottie agreed as Amy looked and saw that he was more focused on Abigail than the view. Amy elbowed him hard in the ribs. "Ow! What was that for?" Scottie yelped, tearing his focus away from Abigail and now onto Amy.

She rolled her eyes and crossed her arms across her chest. *She is lucky I did not toss her overboard.* They heard a screeching scream from under them, and they all looked down at the cart below. It was Mari-Kate screaming at the top of her lungs in fear. Ricky and Avey were rocking their cart as if swinging on a swing set.

"STOP IT!" Mari-Kate yelled as she gripped the bar in the middle of the cart with all her might. "Guys, cut it out. You are scaring her to death," Miranda exclaimed, pleading with them.

"Ricky, y'all stop, she is really scared!" Abigail yelled from above.

"We are just having fun, jeez you guys," one of the guys snickered.

"Well, it isn't fun to everyone here," Miranda said as she motioned over to Mari-Kate who was pale as a ghost.

The guys stopped when they saw she was almost in tears. "I am sorry. We were just kidding around, we didn't mean to upset you so badly," Ricky calmly said in a sincere voice as he realized how traumatized his date was. He pulled her back in the seat slowly.

By now the ride was over and was stopping every few minutes to let the passengers off. Once they all exited, Amy rushed to check on Mari-Kate. They walked ahead of the group murmuring and whispering. You could not see Mari-Kate's face, but she was crying. “I think y'all went a little too far,” Miranda said, looking over to Avey.

“Y’all know she has a fear of heights,” Abigail insisted, “Did you think she was going to take that lightly?”

Ricky rubbed his head with his hat, “We honestly weren't thinking at the moment. I will apologize and calm her down.” He sped up to catch up with her. “Amy, can I talk to Mari-Kate please?” He asked as he finally got up beside them.

“I think you have done enough!” she said with a dagger-throwing stare.

“It's okay,” Mari-Kate assured her.

“Well, I am right behind you if you need me,” Amy gasped, giving Ricky another hateful glare, and turned back to join the others.

Ricky put his arm around her, and they started talking as the others followed behind them, far enough to give them privacy, but close enough to where they could all stay together. “Is she okay?” Miranda asked Amy when she returned to the rest of them.

“As okay as expected,” Amy snared.

Scottie went to put his arm around her, but she just jolted her shoulder away. “What's with you?” He asked her.

“As if you have no idea,” she claimed in her sarcastic tone, with her eyes squinted.

“I don't,” he claimed as he shrugged. They all walked on quietly for the next few minutes watching Ricky try to console and make up with Mari-Kate. When they saw her laugh, they knew that they had worked it out, and things were back to normal.

They went on to ride some more rides starting with the Himalayas which everyone enjoyed. They all rode it screaming with their arms raised, cheering for it to go faster and faster. Then onto the Sea Dragon, a ship that swings back and forth. The back seats are the perfect seats because they take you so high that it feels as if you can reach up and touch the sky. As they were walking off the exit ramp, Xavier inquired, “Can we ride the zipper now? I have been patient long enough, and I know we should be good by now."

The girls squinted their noses at each other. "I don't want to ride it," Mari-Kate mumbled, "the Ferris wheel was enough with you two boys."

"I will stay with her and wait for y'all," Amy added. The girls stood side by side with their arms looped as if to say 'you aren't separating us'.

"Yeah, I think one is too much for me. I am not going to ride either." Miranda agreed.

Xavier looked over to Abigail, "What about you?" he teased.

"I am not so sure, myself," Abigail responded as she observed the ride with its twirling baskets.

"I can't believe you are bailing out on me. I never saw you as a chicken." Xavier challenged her.

"What did you say?" Abigail gasped as she smacked his arm playfully.

Xavier laughed "You heard me. You're being a chicken."

"I am not!" Abigail protested. "If you are scared to ride by yourself then I will ride with you," she offered in a teasing manner.

"WHAT? I am not scared to ride by myself. You are the one who doesn't want to ride, and you are calling me scared," Xavier declared.

"Fine let's do this," Abigail affirmed as she started walking toward the line.

"Ricky, are you up for it?" Scottie questioned as he took off after Xavier and Abigail.

"No. I am going to stay with the girls to make sure they are alright." Ricky said as he stood by Mari-Kate.

"I will ride with you, Scottie," Avey answered as he took off in a slight jog to catch up with him.

"We will stay close by. Just call when y'all are off and we will meet up again." Miranda called out as they ran to get in line.

“Are you sure you can handle this?” Xavier teased Abigail as they stood in line, waiting for their turn.

“I think the real question is, are you ready? Since you insisted on needing someone to ride with you,” she remarked.

“I'm not scared. I just didn't want to ride with a stranger.” Xavier responded, “I can handle you upchucking on me, but not a total stranger.”

They both laughed. The ride was now boarding passengers and the line started to move.

“You guys ready!” Scottie inquired as they were the next ones to get on.

“Of course!” Xavier exclaimed.

“We will see y'all soon,” Avey said as Xavier and Abigail were getting strapped into their seats in the small, wired basket.

One by one each basket is filled with passengers as it slowly turns, and the baskets slowly rock back and forth.

“Have you ever ridden this before?” Xavier asked as they were waiting for the ride to begin.

“Nope. This will be my first.” She confessed.

“Are you serious? I was sure that you would have ridden this before,” he said in disbelief.

Abigail shook her head, reassuring him that she had not. The basket must have been filled because the ride was starting to turn at a steady pace without stopping. After the second or third time around, it picked up speed and the baskets began to spin in a circular motion. You could hear all the screams over the music that was being blared. It seemed like it was longer than it was, although it only lasted a few minutes or more. As fast as they started spinning the baskets, it slowed to just a rock once more. Once they all exited, Abigail grabbed onto the closest rail she could find to lean on. Scottie saw that she was turning a green color.

“I think she is going to upchuck.” Avey cautioned as Scottie sped to her.

“Are you okay?” He asked as he got to her side.

"I am not feeling so good," Abigail answered as she slid down to the pavement and pulled her legs to her chest.

"Just sit for a while. I will go get you a drink." Xavier urged as he ran to the nearest concession stand. "I need a large Sprite, please," he told the concessionaire as he grabbed a five from his wallet. The concessionaire returned with the drink and gave him his change. He shoved the change in his pocket as he jogged back over to where Abigail was still resting on the ground with her head resting on her knees.

"I am sorry, I shouldn't have provoked you to ride it with me," Xavier confessed as he handed her the drink.

"I make my own decisions. It was all fun and games. No one can take the blame for my choices, except me," she remarked as she pushed the straw into her drink and took a sip.

While they waited, Avey called the others to let them know they were off the ride and their location. He informed them of Abigail's illness and that they wanted to give her time to rest before going on to something else. They all stood for a few minutes in silence letting her rest.

"Abigail, you shouldn't have ridden that," Miranda said as she came upon her.

"Do you need anything to eat or drink?" Ricky inquired.

"No thanks. Xavier bought me a Sprite," she answered, lifting the glass that was sitting at her feet. "Guys, I think I am going to call it a night and head home," she uttered as she stumbled to her feet.

"I don't think you should drive in your condition," Miranda insisted. "Let me drive you home, and Avey can follow us." Avey nodded in agreement.

"No, I will be fine," Abigail stubbornly grunted.

"No, you will not," Scottie stated in concern.

"I am just nauseated, that is all. Not like I am disorientated or something. If I get sick, I will just pull over, and wait till I am good to drive again," Abigail appealed.

"No, I will drive you home," Scottie spoke up. "Ricky do you and Mari-Kate mind giving Amy a ride home?" he questioned as he looked over his shoulder at them.

"Not at all, man," Ricky expressed.

Now Amy was upset, and Mari-Kate could see it all over her face. "Why can't we just follow you there and give you a lift back home," Miranda volunteered. Doing her best not to let another night end like this. She wasn't ready to hear any of Amy's jealous rage and listen to her vent tonight.

"No, I did this by encouraging her to ride with me. I should be the one to take her home. No need for all your dates to end abruptly," Xavier interrupts.

"NO! I am bringing her home, and I will call you later, Amy, when she is settled," Scottie declared.

"This is--" Abigail started to speak, but was interrupted by Scottie, "You aren't driving yourself. I have my mind made up, so no use arguing with me about it."

He grabbed her drink from her hand, wrapped his arm around her waist to assist her, and they both started heading to the car. "You are treating me like a little girl. I can walk you know," Abigail sassed.

"Fine, I will let you walk by yourself but once you start wobbling, I am going to help you," Scottie grumbled. As soon as he let her go, she started stumbling like someone just getting off a merry-go-round. He grabbed her once more. "See you aren't fine," he corrected her. She gave him a look while they walked to find the car. His arm was comfortably around her waist to hold her steady. The walk seemed to be forever, and Abigail was feeling worse by the minute. "Wait, can we stop? I don't feel so good."

Scottie stopped and looked at her with a concerned face, "do you need your drink?" Abigail shook her head and bent over in agony. "What is it? What can I do?" Before he could ask another question, she hurled all over his shoes. "Ugh, Abby! Do you feel better now?" Abigail motioned for her drink without responding. "Are you sure you need more?"

She shook her hand as if to say, 'give it to me'. Scottie handed her the sprite. Abigail sipped enough of it to wash the nasty taste from her mouth, then spit. "That helped a little," she explained, "but I'm still nauseous and my head is pounding."

"We're close to your car," Scottie reassured her. "Cool off for a second," he said, handing her the Sprite to hold while he took his favorite Converse off to throw in the nearest trash bin.

"I'm sorry," Abigail apologized, "for ruining your shoes."

"No worries," Scottie said, walking back to her from the bin. "I'll get a new pair or something. Are you feeling well enough to get to the car?"

"Yes, the sooner we get to the car the sooner I can get home to rest," Abigail answered, "but I think I may be able to walk from here on my own." They finally made it to her car, and she gave him the keys. The ride home was silent as she leaned back in the passenger seat on her side.

He pulled up and parked her car under the carport, killed the ignition and got out. He walked around and slowly opened the door to make sure she doesn't fall out. She was asleep. He picked her up and carried her to the door. Knocking slightly with his foot. Mrs. Mia answered suddenly. "We were expecting you," she said as she swung the door wide for them both to come through, "Miranda called and let us know to be expecting y'all. How is she, and where are your shoes?" she inquired as she noticed that he was only in socks.

"She didn't make it very far in the parking lot when she was overwhelmed with the urge to vomit, and my shoes got the worst of it," Scottie chuckled.

"Oh my," she laughed. "I am sorry."

"It's okay." Scottie replied.

"You can just lay her on the couch." Mrs. Mia added.

“No ma'am. I can carry her up to her room. Just in case she wakes up, then she wouldn’t have to climb the stairs,” he expressed with concern. She moved over for him to have access to the stairway. He lugged her up the stairs as if it was no struggle at all. Once they got to her room, he laid her down on her bed. Mrs. Mia took off her shoes. Scottie took the blanket at the end of her bed and covered her.

“Thank you for taking care of her, Scottie,” Mrs. Mia whispered as they walked out, closing the door behind them.

“No worries. I always have and I always will,” he stated as they reached the top of the stairs. She smiled gratefully at him.

“Arnold is going to give you a ride home.” Mrs. Mia said.

“No need, I was going to walk home. It’s not that far,” he pleaded. “I hate to put y'all out.”

“You made sure our daughter arrived to us safely, and I am going to do the same,” Mr. Arnold greeted him with a handshake at the bottom of the stairs. “Besides it is dark and after 9:30 PM, there is no need for you to be walking home this late alone.”

“Thank you, sir,” Scottie nodded with a smile.

*Graduation (Friends Forever) - Vitamin C*

# CHAPTER 9

## Class of 2014

*It is crazy to think school will be over in just a few more weeks. I will graduate!* Abigail thought as she hit the off button for her alarm. "I sure hope we will all stay in touch with each other, and not only see each other just at reunions," she murmured out loud to herself as she sat up on the side of her bed. They became her best friends when she moved to Savannah, and she doesn't want graduation to change that. Graduation brings so much change in life that she doesn't want to lose her friends in the process as well.

She grabbed her clothes and headed to the bathroom to get dressed for the day. Today, the committee was to have a meeting to go over the final details once more, and make sure everything was already for Saturday night. She felt butterflies in her stomach. "Just my nerves" she sighed, hoping to let all the fluttering feeling escape in her exhale. She put her hair in a high ponytail and brushed her teeth. She walked down the stairs to find her mom in the kitchen, sitting at the bar and going over her weekly planner.

"Good morning." She greeted her mom with a kiss on the forehead.

"Good morning." She replied, not looking up from her planner. "Saturday is going to be busy starting at 10:00. We are scheduled for hair and makeup at the salon."

"Yes, ma'am," Abigail answered as she grabbed an apple from the fruit bowl and took a bite. She gripped it between her teeth as she swung her backpack on her shoulder. She grabbed her keys off the counter.

"I am in a hurry. We have a committee meeting this morning before homeroom." Abigail spoke as she leaned down and gave her mom another kiss on the forehead.

"Have a great day. Love you." She said.

"I love you, too. You have a great day as well!" Abigail stated as she closed the door.

Abigail arrived at school ten minutes before the meeting. *Enough time to grab some orange juice from the cafeteria before I head to the meeting,* she thought, looking at her watch. She drank the orange juice, finished her toast and headed to the student council's office.

Everyone was at the table chatting when she arrived.

"Good morning, everyone." Abigail chirped, taking her seat at the round table. She pulled out her binder and placed it in front of her. The meeting was brief and successful.

"This prom is going to be amazing," Sara affirmed as they all headed for the door.

"I am a little emotional about all of it," Abigail confessed.

"Emotional?" Mari-Kate questioned.

"Prom is the last step before graduation, and I am afraid of the changes that come after that. It leaves me in a whirlwind of emotions." Abigail shared.

"We are going to college together, so at least seeing each other every day won't change," Miranda said, trying to comfort her friend.

"Yes, we will, but what about everyone else?" Abigail asked when she opened her locker.

"I am sure we will all keep in touch," Sara said.

"You're not going to get rid of me that easily," Scottie whispered in Abigail's ear as he leaned in to open his locker. Abigail jumped in surprise, startled by his appearance. She didn't realize he had been listening to their conversation, but also, being so close to him made her heart skip several beats.

"Scottie, you scared me!" she smiled her sweet smile at him, trying to cover up her blushed cheeks. Hoping her friends would think it was caused by him scaring her and not the closeness of the two.

"Yeah, you are so easy to scare," he smiled. Oh, his smile could make her darkest day feel like the brightest summer day. She turned her head hoping he couldn't read her thoughts from her face.

"Always got jokes." She giggled. "But seriously you guys aren't worried that after school we will lose touch and rarely see each other?"

"Nope," Mari-Kate assured her.

"Well, I don't think it would be a bad thing for some of us to get space from one another if you ask me." Amy snorted.

Of course, she wouldn't be too far behind Scottie. She was so much like the little puppy dog that followed him around. So scared someone else will steal his attention away from her. Abigail shut her locker and turned around, catching Amy's glare.

"It is too early for your mess." Miranda snarled.

Amy rolled her eyes, "Let's go, Scottie, I am going to be late for my homeroom class."

"What? The little puppy can't walk by herself?" Miranda snarled.

"What did you say?" Amy asked. She had heard Miranda perfectly, but being the girl she was, she always made things difficult.

"You heard me," Miranda said as she glared right back at Amy.

"Come on Miranda, let's get to class," Abigail said soothingly, trying to mellow out the tension between them.

"Who needs to be walked now?" Amy snorted.

"Scottie, you better pull her leash before I show her who the big dog is," Miranda said firmly, with her fist tightly shut by her side.

"Calm down both of you! My goodness it is way too early for y'all to be at each other's throats already," he insisted as he grabbed Amy by the arm and pulled her in the direction of her homeroom.

"This isn't over!" Amy shouted back to Miranda.

"Ooh, I am so scared," Miranda said, shaking as if she was afraid.

"Come on." Abigail grabbed Miranda and turned her in the opposite direction. "Why do you let her get you like that?"

"How can you not? You know she was talking about you and Scottie with her little remark." Miranda said.

"Yes, I know. How could I not with the glare she was giving me." Abigail stated.

"I still cannot believe Scottie has been with her after all these years. I was sure she would have been gone after the way she has acted towards you."

"He loves her, Miranda. We may not like her, but we do need to accept her for Scottie's sake." They took their seats in their pre-calculus class with Mrs. Harper.

"I don't have to be nice to her. I am not a fake friend, you know I speak my mind, and you are so mistaken about who he loves. Either you are blind or you don't just want to see it." Miranda stated as she put her backpack down by her seat.

Abigail set her bag down and leaned back in her chair. She giggled "I have no idea what you are talking about, and I assure you I am not blind. I do know that I am surprised that you two have not come to blows yet with all the constant bickering you two do with each other."

"She wouldn't know what hit her if we came to blows. It is all because of you that I keep my hands to myself, if not she would have had what was coming to her. I promise you that." Miranda turned in her seat to face the front of the classroom.

"Well, for her sake I hope that never happens." Abigail insisted. The bell rang for class to start, and Miranda just raised her eyebrows and shrugged her shoulders.

"One day though, she is going to go too far. Mark my words." Miranda whispered.

"She isn't worth getting in trouble over. Be the bigger person, or in your case, 'the big dog'," Abigail whispered. She tried but failed to suppress her laugh. Miranda looked at her, face dropping for a moment, but she couldn't help but smile as well.

Scottie and Xavier were sitting on the bleachers during practice, enjoying not having to participate in the activities anymore since they were about to graduate.

"Hey, Scottie, can I ask you something?" Xavier asked.

"Sure. What's up?" He replied.

"Well, you know I don't have a date for prom, right?" Xavier stated.

"Yeah, but I thought you said you wanted to go solo so that you could dance with whoever you wanted." Scottie remarked.

"Well, that was not so true. There is someone I want to ask, but I don't know if I can or if she will even say yes. She might already have a date to the prom." Xavier explained.

"What is that supposed to mean? You are the center on the football team, and you are a great guy. Not so bad looking either, not as good looking as me, but somewhere in the running for sure." He gave Xavier a friendly slap on the back.

"Yeah. Easy for you to say when you are my best friend." Xavier commented.

"Well, do I know her?" Scottie asked.

"Yes, that is why I am scared to ask her to go with me." Xavier urged.

"Bro, you can't ask my girlfriend to the prom." Scottie snapped in.

"No, I would never want to do anything with Amy. It is Abigail" Xavier stated.

"Abby?" Scottie asked in a shocked tone. "Why are you asking me if you can ask Abby to the prom?"

"I know y'all are close, and I just don't want to overstep." Xavier explained.

"No worries. We are just friends. Of course, you can ask her. I wouldn't trust anyone else to treat her right." Scottie assured.

"Do you know if she has a date?" Xavier inquired.

"This is Abby we are talking about. I am sure she has shot down every guy in school who has asked her." Scottie chuckled. "You know how she is."

"Yes, that is why I am so scared to ask her. What if she says no?" Xavier added.

"What if she says yes?" Scottie asked, placing his right hand on his knee, "you won't know unless you ask."

"I guess you are right. You are okay if I ask her?" Xavier inquired again.

"Like I said, I would not like her to be escorted to the prom by anyone else," Scottie stated.

"Great, then it is settled. I will go to her house and ask her tonight." Xavier smiled.

Abigail was in her room when her mom called downstairs. "Xavier is here to see you."

"Yes ma'am, be right there," Abigail shouted out her bedroom door. *What is Xavier doing here?* She questioned as she started walking down the stairs.

Xavier was standing in the lobby by the front door. He was wearing a nice button-down top with khakis. He had his hair with the wave look in the front. She could smell his polo sport cologne before she reached the bottom step.

"Hey, Xavier. You are looking sharp. What's going on?" Abigail stated as she greeted him with a hug.

“Well, I came to see you about something. Is there a place we can talk?” Xavier asked as he nervously placed his hands in his pockets.

“Sure. Let's go sit by the pool in the back.” Abigail said as she led him to the back door. “Is everything okay?” She asked as he opened the back door for her.

“Yeah. I just wanted to ask you something. Everything is fine.” He stated, closing the door behind them. Abigail led him to the sofa underneath the cabana by the pool. There is a nice breeze blowing, so it is not so bad to sit outside on a May afternoon. “I want you to know that I understand if your answer is no, and I will respect your answer,” Xavier said as they took their seats next to each other on the sofa.

“I have never known you not to be respectful, Xavier,” Abigail said as she cuddled into the cushions of the sofa.

“I am going to just come out and ask you. Better to just get it over with,” he said, rubbing his hands nervously on his legs.

“Just ask me, it can’t be that bad. You don’t have any reason to be so nervous. We have known each other for a long time,” she reassured.

“Abigail, will you go to the prom with me?” Xavier asked rather quickly as if he was trying to beat some type of record.

Abigail was sort of shocked. That was the last thing she expected him to ask her. Xavier saw the look on her face. “You don’t have to answer, I see it on your face. It is fine, I knew I shouldn’t have asked. You are way out of my league.” Xavier frowned and stood to leave before she could respond.

“Xavier, that is not true. You aren’t going to let me respond?” she inquired, pulling his arm, and making him sit back down.

“There is no need for me to. I can see it all over your face.” He answered with a shy giggle.

“Listen. I am just shocked because I haven’t even thought about that. It was the last thing I expected. I guess I have been so busy with organizing it, with finals, graduation, and everything else that I never even stopped to notice that no one has asked me. Yet, to think that was your question." Abigail explained. "My answer is yes; I will be your date for prom."

"Really! That is awesome! Can you tell me the color of your dress so that I can get the corsage to match?" He now asked in an exciting tone.

"Well, I will be easy to match because my dress is black, and my shoes are gold to match the décor. Would you like to hang out and stay for dinner?"

Xavier was so happy that his smile would not leave his face. "Sure. I don't have anything planned for this evening."

They played several games of pool before dinner time and had a great time with one another. After dinner, everyone gathered in the den to visit for a couple of hours before Xavier headed home.

Tuesday was the seniors' last day of school. Abigail was full of emotions. She knew that this day would come but was not emotionally prepared. They all shared many tears throughout the morning. Emptying their lockers brought it home for all of them. This would be the last time they would gather at their locker before and after class to discuss how much homework they had or what grade they had on their test.

Lunch was the end of their day, so they decided to just go to a restaurant to eat instead of the cafeteria. They all met at Maple Street Biscuits, which is one of their favorite places to hang out together. They sat in their usual spot upstairs, and reminisced for hours over their memories together.

As Abigail drove home, she cried. She was hurting at the thought of not being able to see everyone every day like the last 4 years. Sure, they didn't see each other every weekend, but she knew that Monday would come for them to discuss their weekend trips, events, etc. *This* won't *happen at our lockers anymore. Will we ever have time to meet up like this again once everyone starts college and their jobs? Scottie will be away at college. Will he forget about me? Please don't let him come back engaged, or worse married.* Tears streamed down her face. *It can't be.*

When she arrived home, it took her a few minutes to gather herself before getting out of the car. She shut the front door behind her and called out, "I'll be in my room. It has been a long emotional day," as she headed up the stairs.

"Okay, dear," Mr. Arnold answered.

"I am here if you need to talk," Mrs. Mia said.

"Thank you," Abigail replied.

She FaceTimed Isabella and Brook. They all shared their emotions and feelings toward graduating, and how much their lives were about to change in the next few weeks.

You are the Reason – Calum Scott

# CHAPTER 10

## Prom

The days flew by, which was a shock to Abigail as she thought it would drag by since they weren't having school. Saturday was here and it was going to be another emotional roller coaster. Abigail didn't know whether to be happy or sad, and the morning had just begun. She was at the salon getting her nails, hair, and make-up done.

"Are you excited about tonight," Mary the cosmetologist asked, as she washed her hair to prepare for her trim and styling.

"I am, but also nervous, too," Abigail confessed.

"It will be a blast, I am sure. You have nothing to be nervous about." She assured her as she massaged the shampoo into her scalp. One of her favorite things about going to the salon for trim was the scalp massage while they shampooed her hair.

"Do you have a date?" Mary asked as she began the rinse.

"Yes, it was kind of the last minute," Abigail giggled.

"That is guys for you, they are good at procrastinating. Wait till the very last second or moment to do something." Mary snickered.

"Well to be honest, I forgot that I didn't have a date." Abigail stated.

"Girl, how can you forget that?" Mary snapped as she lifted her head to place the towel over Abigail's head and start drying her hair. "That is an important detail, don't you think?" She asked as she looked around to see Abigail eye to eye.

"Yes, but I was so busy with organizing and planning it that I didn't even realize it until he asked me," Abigail laughed.

"You have a better attitude about it than I would have if my boyfriend waited till the last second to ask me to the prom." She continued.

"Oh, he isn't my boyfriend. We have been friends since junior high. He is kind of shy, so I am sure he had to work up the nerve to ask," Abigail commented, taking up for Xavier and reminding her that she wasn't dating anyone.

"Well, I would rather have him ask me than not ask at all," Mary suggested as she grabbed the scissors from her jar of disinfectant. She started parting Abigail's hair to start the trimming.

Abigail drifted off into her thoughts, which filled her mind with all that she had left to do before 3:00 PM. Xavier and the others were going to arrive at 4:00 to pick her up in the limo that Amy's parents had rented for the group to ride to the prom in.

Then they were going to take pictures downtown at the Davenport House with its dual cascading stairs for the front entrance. In the foyer, you are welcomed by the beautiful ivory, arched doorway that is supported by two columns, and the enchanted stairway that can be viewed behind them. A large, gorgeous garden in the rear with a large fountain in the center, and a koi pond near the back of the garden. The amazing, historic home will make a glamorous backdrop for their pictures.

Then off to grab a bite at Ruth Chris's Steakhouse before they head to their destination, the Prom.

She was brought back to reality as Mary asked her what type of hairstyle she wanted for her big night. She opened a magazine to show a beautiful style with a cascading ponytail of curls coming down on the right side. "This will look gorgeous!" Mary assured her. She grabbed a brush and began styling.

Abigail was deep in thought running over the last-minute to-do lists when Mary turned her around to look in the mirror. It was gorgeous just as Mary stated. Abigail's face said it all as her smile glowed on her face. "I love it!"

"Oh, Abigail, you look so beautiful." Mrs. Mia uttered. "Thank you, Mary. You did an amazing job!" Mary nodded in gratitude as Mrs. Mia slipped a $10.00 bill into her tip jar. "Let's get your makeup done, and then we can head over to the mani-pedi spa," Mrs. Mia suggested.

"Sounds great," Abigail agreed.

She sat in the chair as Michelle started applying her makeup. Abigail drifted off in her thoughts again wondering what she should order for dinner. She didn't care to eat in front of other people. Just felt awkward to her at times. Maybe a small salad or appetizer just to hold her over until after prom. After all, there would be snack foods there that she could munch on all night.

Before she knew it, Michelle was done with her makeup. Michelle also did a good job with keeping all natural colors just as Abigail requested. She didn't like makeup caked up on her face. She felt as though she was a clown headed for a circus or something. Just keep it natural and you can never go wrong. She chose the color, sweetheart, which is a soft pale pink, for her nail polish, then took a seat at the nail counter for her manicure, and would finish up with a pedicure. Before she knew, it was 1:30 PM, and Heather was finishing up her toenails.

"Can we run through a drive-thru for a bite on the way home?" Abigail asked.

"Sure, do you have anything in particular in mind?" Mr. Mia asked.

"A quick burger stop sounds good to me." She answered.

"Sounds good." Mrs. Mia agreed as she moved to the cashier's stand to pay for their services.

They made it home a little after 2:00 PM. Abigail ran up to her room to finish getting dressed. She sprayed her perfume,

Forever and Ever Dior, on her pulse points, so that the fragrance could linger if she did get close to someone. She stood in front of the mirror to take in her attire. She wore a romantic black lace mermaid dress, with an illusion neckline, and a princess-seamed sweetheart bodice with short cap sleeves that were trimmed with scalloped eyelash details. It was a maxi length that fell from the waist into a flattering mermaid hem with flaring godets. It contoured her petite and toned frame. Her Jessica Simpson Rayli2 gold shoes made her look even taller. She adjusted the curls that had been misplaced when she put on her dress. Before she knew it, Xavier was knocking on the door. As she came down the stairs, he was standing at the bottom of the steps, wearing a Paul Malone formal gold tuxedo vest and black suit. He had his hair styled nicely with the fade cut. He had on his famous Polo Sport cologne that she could smell as she drew closer to the bottom of the steps. Xavier took a deep breath, captivated by how gorgeous she looked. Her parents were standing in the entranceway to the den from the lobby. Mrs. Mia gasped, "Oh, Abigail. You look beautiful." Mr. Arnold was too emotional to speak.

Xavier was the first to speak. "Abigail, you look amazing," as he held out his hand to assist her down the last few steps. Xavier placed the corsage on her left wrist. It was a perfect match for their attire. He had a black and gold rose with a gold glitter ribbon that sparkled in the light. Just enough black and gold leaves and ribbon to make it full. It fit her small wrist perfectly.

"Oh, it's so pretty, Xavier. Thank you." She said.

"Do y'all have time for me to take a few pictures?" Mrs. Mia asked.

"Yes, ma'am. Only a few, the others are outside waiting." Abigail replied. After what felt like twenty pictures, they headed for the door. Xavier held the door as she hugged her parents' bye. As they exited the house, Xavier held his right arm out to escort her to the car.

Scottie was standing outside the limo looking like the chauffeur, though mighty handsome. He was wearing a tuxedo that was a close match to Xavier's, just the vest and tie had a different design. He had his hair cut short on the sides, but the top was filled with curls. He had on his pilot sunglasses that hid his beautiful brown eyes. *I am sure I could see the green in them if he didn't have the glasses on* she thought to herself. As they approached him, she caught his Armani Code cologne blow over with the breeze. She took a deep breath to collect herself. He always smelled so good. Abigail felt the chill bumps pop up on her arms, and she shivered.

"Are you cold? Do I need to grab you a jacket before we leave?" Xavier asked.

"No, I am good. Thank you." She replied as she clasped her right hand at the bend of his arm.

She looked back at the limo. If Abigail didn't know any better, she would think he was blushing. *Must be the heat out here* she told herself.

Miranda shouted, "Watch out men, the heartbreaker is out and about tonight!"

Abigail blushed and shook her head.

After a nice dinner, they arrived at the prom. Each boy escorted their girl into the beautiful auditorium with cathedral ceilings lightly lit with candles and white lights. It was decorated beautifully with black, gold, and white curtains that matched the table decorations and plate settings. Sara did such a wonderful job with the designs. It took them a long time to get it decorated but walking in with everything all set up made Abigail feel overwhelmed with joy.

They were all dancing when Scottie saw the way that Xavier was looking at Abigail. A little amount of jealousy crept over him. He wanted so badly to go and ask to interrupt, but he couldn't do that to both of his best friends. He and Abigail had been nothing but friends after all these years. She has not once shown any interest in him, *why ruin everything now*? She just looked so beautiful tonight. He hadn't seen her dressed up like this before. Sure, the homecoming dances and such, but that was just casual dress. This is how he pictured her looking on her wedding day. *Would I even be invited? Will we remain close after graduation? Could I live with her marrying someone else?* Abigail laughed at something Xavier had said. Oh, how he loved to hear her laugh, but he didn't like it when another guy made her laugh. Her eyes sparkled when she laughed at his hilarious ways. The way her lips would curl into a smile as she greeted him made him want to gently press his lips to hers. His jealousy was starting to take over his thoughts which in turn was raising his emotions. *If I am this way with my best friend on a date with Abigail. How am I going to feel when someone else walks her down the aisle?* He was starting to sweat, and without him even realizing, he was gripping Amy's hand tighter.

When Amy's voice snapped him back into reality, "Are you okay?"

"What? I can barely hear you over the music playing. Let's go sit down for a moment." Scottie insisted, trying to put as much distance between Abigail, Xavier, and himself. "What were you saying?" He asked Amy as they sat down at the table that was reserved for their group.

"I was asking if you were ok. You were squeezing my hand pretty hard." She inquired.

"Oh, sorry. Yeah, I am fine." He stated.

"Are you as excited as I am that in just a few months we will be attending college together? Just the two of us, no one else to interfere." She added.

"Interfere? What do you mean by that? I am going to miss my friends and the football team." He looked back over at the dance floor at their friends dancing. "And what about Mari-Kate? She is going to Ohio State as well, so it isn't like you and her won't be spending time together." He was overlooking the interference that Amy was calling out, Abigail.

"Of course, we are going to do things together, but Mari-Kate isn't one to push and prod to be her bodyguard, or whatever some damsel in distress would need." She cut in.

He sharply turned to look at her. "You don't want to start this tonight, Amy. I am only here because you wanted me to be. I would rather be at home playing Call of Duty than sweating in this penguin suit," he reminded her.

"This is our last night together as seniors in high school, Scottie. I thought you would be happy to spend it with me." Amy replied.

"Maybe you would want to try and enjoy rather than pick a fight." He took a sip of his punch and peered at her over the rim of the glass.

"I am not picking a fight. I am just stating the obvious." Amy fired back.

"Avey and Miranda are coming, so change the subject." Scottie stated.

"Some of those interruptions I was speaking of." She answered.

Scottie leaned in close as if he was going to kiss her, "I have heard enough of your bickering tonight. Let's enjoy it, okay," he whispered in her ear, so only she could hear. When he went to kiss her cheek, she turned quickly away from him.

"Are we interrupting?" Avey asked as he saw Amy roll her eyes. Thankfully Miranda was grabbing her cup and didn't see her. "We can go sit somewhere else and give y'all some privacy."

"That is not necessary. Everything that needs to be said has been said," Scottie said as he glared at Amy to not start anything else.

"Oh, thank you. I am burning up and need to sit for a moment," Miranda stated as she drank some more of her punch.

"Xavier and Abigail look as if they are having fun," aiming to hit two targets at once, Scottie and Amy.

"Yeah, don't they though," Scottie said as nonchalantly as possible, hoping no one saw right through him.

"They would make a cute couple. They sure have danced around for a long time," Avey insinuated.

"Really?" Scottie asked, "I guess I have never paid much attention."

"Xavier has always liked her but feels that he is out of her league. Everyone knows how Abigail is about dating. She would rather lay up with a stack of books all weekend than go out on a date," Avey stated. "I have tried to convince him to ask her, but it goes in one ear and out the other."

"I know what you mean. I had to almost twist his arm to ask her to prom," Scottie agreed.

"Why did you ask him to take her to prom?" Amy snarled.

"I didn't. He was talking about asking her in practice last week, and I had to spend all period talking him into going through with it," Scottie answered.

Everyone hushed as they came to join the group when the song ended.

"I am having a blast! But I feel out of shape," Abigail laughed.

"Me too," Xavier agreed. "Would you like me to get us some punch?" He pulled Abigail's seat out for her.

"Yes, you may want to make it a double," she teased as she sat down.

"Will do. Does anyone else need anything?" Xavier asked.

Everyone shook their heads, and he turned to go to the drink table.

Abigail picked up a napkin from the table and started fanning herself, "man, it is hot in here. I think we should have invested in some hand fans for everyone."

"That would have been nice," Miranda agreed. "We should tell the Junior committee so they can make sure to add it to their list for their prom night."

"Great idea!" Mari-Kate stated as she and Ricky sat down. "I can call Sheila tomorrow and tell her to bring it to their next meeting."

"Yeah," Abigail and Miranda both nodded.

Xavier sat down and handed Abigail her drinks. She thanked him and drank almost all of the first cup in one sip. "Thank you! My mouth was so dry."

They all danced and enjoyed each other's company since this would be the last time together in high school. The hours passed by quickly, and the announcement for everyone to gather around the stage to hear the results for the prom King and Queen.

"Finally, I have been waiting for this all night. Let's go, my King," Amy said with confidence as though she knew the results already. She grabbed Scottie's arm and almost dragged him to the dance floor.

"Hey, don't speak too soon. Others could have been voted Queen and King," Miranda insinuated, tugging on Avey's arm.

"That may be, but with me being a captain of the cheer squad and Scottie is quarterback and captain of the football team, I highly don't see that likely," Amy scolded.

"We will see about that," Mari-Kate chimed in. "I think Ricky and I have this in the bag." She looked up and smiled at Ricky.

"For sure, baby girl," Ricky agreed with her, returning a smile.

Mrs. Harris, the principal, asked everyone to calm down, so they could hear. The crowd hushed to just mumbles. They brought the crown and tiara closer to her. Coach James stood in a nice black suit with a gold tie at the microphone with the big gold envelope in his hand to announce the king. There came silence over the crowd as everyone waited with anticipation for the prom king's name to be called. "The winner of this year's prom king goes to," he paused as someone gave a drum roll with a spare drum. "Scottie Harmon! Come on up and claim your crown," he announced.

Amy squealed with excitement, "I told you!"

Mari-Kate shrugged her shoulders. "You're still my queen," Ricky said as he looked down at her and squeezed his arms around her waist, hugging her to himself.

"Thank you. You are my king," she spoke softly with a smile.

Everyone cheered as the coach crowned Scottie King. Ms. Smith, their English teacher, took the stage, wearing a long, haltered top, sequenced, mermaid black dress that made her look stunning. She was one of those teachers that all the boys drooled over. She had her short blonde hair pulled with curls, cascading around her small bun at the nape of her neck. All the boys started whistling and cheering even louder as she approached the microphone. "Calm down boys," she spoke softly in her sweet voice. Coach James motioned for them to lower their voices for her to speak. Again, a hush went over the crowd for her to announce the prom queen. Amy was shaking with excitement as she anticipated the announcement for the queen. As Ms. Smith pulled the card from the envelope, Amy had already started her way to the stage. "The winner of this year's prom queen is… Abigail Whittinger!"

Amy stopped in her tracks. The crowd went wild. Everyone, but Amy.

"How can this be? I am supposed to be queen, not her!" Amy scolded. Her face now flushed red with anger.

Abigail made her way to the stage. Scottie met her at the stairs to assist her up on stage, so she wouldn't fall.

"How did this happen?" she asked as she took his hand.

"Not my circus, not my monkeys," he smirked.

"Oh my, really?" she laughed.

He led her to the front of the stage for them to place the tiara.

"Young ladies and gentlemen, your King and Queen of this year's prom. Scottie Harmon and Abigail Whittinger!" Mrs. Harris announced. "Now we ask that you make room on the dance floor for the King and Queen dance."

Everyone made a huge circle as they made their way off stage. "You are the Reason" by Calum Scott began to play over the speakers. Scottie turned Abigail toward him, giving her a small twirl. He held her left hand and placed his right hand on the small of her back. His closeness was giving her butterflies. The words of the song were playing with her thoughts, and she started to let herself go and let him lead her around the dance floor.

Scottie could smell her perfume as he pulled her a little closer to him. He smiled as they began to dance around the floor. He loved how she just eased into his embrace, if only she knew just how much he cared for her. He listened to the lyrics with her in his embrace... "And I'd climb every mountain and swim every ocean. Just to be with you and fix what I've broken. Oh, 'cause I need you to see that you are the reason." and thinks to himself. *I could not have picked a better song for this very moment. If only I could turn back the clock and make her see that she is the reason. I could love her forever if given the chance. She is so beautiful inside and out. I could just spill my heart to her right here on this floor, but it would cost me so much if she didn't feel the same.* He blinked his eyes to bring himself back to reality. "Abby," he spoke softly.

The sound of his tone made her heart skip beats. "Yes," she answered.

"You look beautiful tonight," still speaking in his soft tone.

"You don't look so bad yourself," she teased to release the urge to get even closer to him. His eyes looking into hers drew her into him like the moon draws the tide from the beach.

They were dancing with each other as though they were all alone in the room, with no audience. It was something they both longed for, just to have a moment like this, but was too scared to take the risk. Because of fear that others could see their feelings displayed with every sway and touch between them while dancing. Everyone was in awe as they watched them on the floor. They were captivated by the chemistry displayed between the two. It was there for everyone to see.

Yes everyone, even Amy. Her blood began to boil. *How could this happen? Who would vote for her to be queen? This is my moment, not hers! She has ruined our night! I cannot wait to get away from this town and her.* "I will have Scottie all to myself, and she will be miles away, out of sight and out of mind," she whispered to herself as she picked up a cup of punch off the drink table. "He will be all mine, and we can move forward with our future together as planned."

Amy was so attuned to her thoughts that she didn't realize the song had ended, and that Scottie and Abigail were headed to the drink table for some punch. "I am so glad that is over! I hate being the center of attention," Abigail sighed. At the same moment, she went to grab her a cup of punch, Amy twirled around, and they collided. Amy's red punch went down the front of her blush pink, laced gown. "AHHHH!" Amy screamed.

"I am so sorry!" Abigail exclaimed as she grabbed napkins to try and dry off her dress.

"DON'T TOUCH ME!" Amy squealed. "YOU ARE SO STUPID!"

"Amy, it was an accident," Scottie said as he pulled her toward him to put space between her and Abigail.

Everyone was turning to look in their direction.

"Oh, it is about to go down," Ricky stated as he nudged Mari-Kate and pointed toward Amy and Abigail.

"Oh no. What has happened now?" Mari-Kate asked. They started walking in their direction.

"You don't have to be so harsh. It was an accident! I didn't know you were going to twirl around as soon as I approached the table." Abigail explained.

"Don't blame this on me! You've been trying to ruin this night since it started!" Amy yelled.

Abigail's mouth dropped slightly open. She looked at Scottie, and then back at Amy. "How in the world have I ruined your night?"

Amy's shrill voice cut through Abigail's soft one, "The crown was supposed to be mine! The dance with Scottie was supposed to be mine! This dress was priceless! You've always been jealous of me, Abigail. Why are you constantly out for me?"

"Ha, jealous of you? Are you out of your mind? What is there to be jealous about?" Abigail fired back. Others at the drinking table had started to watch them like it was a reality show.

"Well, Scottie of course. You have been after him since that summer party of our sophomore year!"

Abigail took a deep breath to try and hold in her anger. "Amy, I have been nothing but nice to you. I held my tongue and tried to be civil for Scottie's sake. You have always blamed me when things don't go your way. I am sorry that you are a spoiled child, who is used to getting her way, but I have no control over things that are out of my hands. Tonight is a great example of that. I didn't choose to be queen but was voted in by others. Honestly, all of it means nothing to me!" Abigail took the crown off her head and held it out to Amy. Scottie's heart dropped at that very moment. "All of it means nothing to me" her words replayed in his mind. The pain of her words cut him deep to the bone. *Did she not feel any of what I just felt as we danced?* He thought to himself. "Here, you want it. You can have it! I am tired of all of it!"

Amy didn't reach for the crown, she glared at Abigail though. If looks could kill… well. Miranda made her way through the crowd that had formed, and Abigail dropped the crown on the ground. She turned to Scottie, who was standing there with his heart in his hands, just glaring at her. His heart was broken, between the fight and what Abigail had said. He wanted to leave. He moved past Abigail and grabbed Amy by the arm. "Come on," he mumbled, pulling her away from Miranda, who was doing everything she could to keep from swinging her fist.

"You better be thankful you pulled that junk here. Why don't you wait till after graduation, and try something like this? Once I walk off that stage with my diploma, nothing will hold me back from you." Miranda shouted out as Amy was being escorted outside by Scottie. Miranda reached down and picked the tiara off the ground and handed it to Abigail. "What happened? Why do I always have to be the one who misses you standing up for yourself?"

Abigail began to trace the tiara with her fingers. Tears started to fill her eyes. She didn't know if it was from her anger or her hurt from Amy accusing her of always interfering.

Xavier walked over and wrapped his arm around Abigail. "Are you okay?"

"Yes," Abigail answered as the tears continued to flow down her face. "I am going to call my mother to come to pick me up."

"What? Don't let her ruin your night! She is just a spoiled brat, who blames everyone if she doesn't get her way," Miranda snapped.

"I am too upset to enjoy the rest of the night," Abigail insisted.

"Well, if you leave, I am going too," Miranda said.

"I can call someone to come get us and bring us home," Xavier offered.

"Thank you, but I just want to go home. I will be fine. I am sorry for ruining tonight," Abigail stated.

"You ruined nothing. I understand," Xavier assured her.

"Everyone here knows who ruined the night," Miranda snapped in.

"I am going outside to call my mom," Abigail said.

"I will walk you out and stay with you until she arrives," Xavier proposed.

"You don't have to. I will be fine. The fresh, night air may help calm me down." She insisted.

"Don't be foolish. I am not going to let a beautiful girl stand outside on the curb, crying alone in the night. Let's go, and I will stay until she picks you up." Xavier exclaimed.

"I am here. Call me if you need to talk, scream, or cry," Miranda offered.

"Thank you," Abigail and Miranda hugged each other. Xavier held out his arm and escorted her outside.

She pulled her phone from her purse and called Mrs. Mia to come pick her up. She scanned around them to make sure Amy was not nearby. When she spotted them, she could tell that Amy and Scottie were fighting. *Do I cause so much trouble for them? How could Amy even think that I am jealous of her? Yes, she wanted to be the one that Scottie loved, but she had come to accept their friendship after all these years. I honestly did not mean to bump into her, and I sure didn't want to be the prom queen.* Tears started to fill her eyes once more. She could feel the warmth of them as they streamed down her cheek.

"Hey, don't do this to yourself," Xavier said in a soft tone. He turned her so that they would be out of her view. "You aren't to blame. It was an accident, and if she can't understand, then that it is all on her." He wrapped his arms around her and pulled her into his embrace. She released a huge breath and let the tears flow. It was nice to be embraced as her heart was so torn. She honestly had no idea how to feel. *Did I just destroy our friendship? He didn't say two words to me. Did he blame me too?*

Scottie looked across the lot and saw Xavier embracing Abigail. It looked as though she was crying. He was so hurt by the comment that Abigail made that he didn't know how to respond. *She doesn't feel the way that I do about her. She literally said it meant nothing to her. I am so stupid for holding on all these years, waiting and hoping for more than a friendship. I must stop here and focus on my future. Whether it be with Amy or not.*

"Where do we stand, Scottie?" Amy's harsh tone snapped him out of his thoughts.

"Huh," he asked.

"You heard me. Where do we stand?" Amy repeated.

"Amy, it has been a long night, and I am tired of fighting with you. If you are ready then call the limo and let's go home." He answered.

"Fine!" Amy said sharply as she reached into the pocket of her dress and pulled out her phone.

Mrs. Mia pulled up to the curb and could tell that Abigail was upset. Xavier opened the door for her. "Call me and let me know you made it home safely."

"Okay," Abigail answered as she clicked her seat belt.

Mrs. Mia thanked Xavier for staying with her until she arrived. They said their goodbyes and watched as Xavier walked back into the building.

"Are you okay, dear," Mrs. Mia asked as she put the car in drive.

"Yes, ma'am. I will be fine. It has been a long night, and I just want a hot bath to soak in for a while." She replied.

As they were reaching the exit of the parking lot. The limo for Scottie and Amy passed them. "Is that the limo y'all were riding in?" Mrs. Mia inquired.

"I am not sure." She leaned her head back against the headrest. She closed her eyes to try and put the night behind her.

"Are you holding a tiara? Did you win prom queen?" Mrs. Mia asked.

"Yes, although I don't wish to discuss it." Abigail replied.

"You should be happy. I am happy for you." Mrs. Mia stated.

"I was happy and also confused when they announced my name, but the night went wrong after Scottie and I danced." She explained.

"Oh no, I assume that someone wasn't happy with that at all." Mrs. Mia continued.

"That is an understatement, and me spilling her punch down the front of her dress didn't help matters." Abigail added.

"How did that happen? I am sure it was an accident." Mrs. Mia inquired.

"It was but you couldn't convince her of that. In fact, from her point of view, I am jealous of her and Scottie. To the point that I have tried to ruin their relationship since the summer splash." Abigail stated.

"That is absurd! You don't have a jealous bone in your body, much less a mean one. I am sure she was just angry and said things she didn't mean." Mrs. Mia said.

"I am not sure. I just want to let it go and move on." She stated.

"I understand sweetie, but I will say that you don't need to let her get the best of you." Mrs. Mia added.

There was silence for the rest of the ride home. When they arrived home, Abigail texted Xavier to let him know she was home, and that she was calling it a night. *A hot soaking bath is just what I need.* She lit some candles, turned on some soft, soothing instrumental music, cut off the lights, and climbed into the tub. She heard her phone notifications going off. *That is probably Miranda just checking up on me. I will call her when I get out.* She closed her eyes and lay there trying to get the eventful night out of her mind. *How do I always get into these predicaments? Why did he not tell her it was her that turned into me? She is right, I am always waiting for him to defend me. Why do I do that? It stops here and now. School is over anyway. He will only be here for a month or so before he moves away. I will just keep to myself, and not speak to him unless spoken to.* Her phone started to ring. *I should have brought it in here with me. I am not even relaxing.* "I might as well just get out. This has been no help," she said as she grabbed her bathrobe. She blew out the candles. She turned on the lamp by her bed and picked up her phone. She had fourteen unread messages. "Oh, my goodness. Do you not get that I just want to be left alone," she said as she unlocked her phone. 'MISSED CALL, SCOTTIE' displayed across her unlocked phone. "Should I call him now or just wait till tomorrow? I would like to know where we stand," she said, holding her finger over the call-back button. She pressed it and heard the line begin to ring. She almost stopped breathing when she heard him say "hello." She almost hung up on him but ignored the urge.

"Abby are you there?" he asked, in a concerned voice.

"Yes." She said.

"I wanted to call and apologize for Amy's behavior tonight." He added.

"You don't owe me an apology." She sat down on the side of her bed. "You do know it was an accident, right?"

"Of course, I do. I know you would never do anything like that deliberately." He continued.

"I was so scared that you were mad at me too, and that is why you didn't say anything to me before you left." She stated.

"How could I be mad at you?" *But how could you not feel what I felt tonight?* He thought to himself. "We all know how dramatic Amy is, and I wanted to get her out of there before things became much worse," he explained. "She was trying to pick a fight with me all night, so I am sorry you received the blunt end of it."

"It's okay. After all these years I am used to it," she said. "You and I are okay though, right?"

"Yes." He agreed.

"That is good to hear. Because of the way things were left at the prom, I thought I had lost you. I—mean our friendship," she corrected herself.

"Abby, you will never lose me," he told her.

Beautiful Things – Benson Boone

# CHAPTER 11

## The Accident

A group of them went out the weekend after graduation to celebrate with dinner and a few games of bowling. They wrapped up the last game at about 9:30 PM because they had a curfew for 10:30 PM. They all stood in the parking lot chatting about how they couldn't wait to get to college where there were no rules or curfews to be followed. Abigail was the first to leave. Scottie and the others stayed behind for a while visiting and playing games of 8 ball pool.

Scottie had just gotten out of the shower and turned on the TV to ESPN when his cell phone rang. *Abby's Dad* was displayed on the ID of the cell as the caller. "Hello," Scottie answered in a questionable tone.

"Hello, Scottie. This is Arnold, Abigail's Dad," Mr. Arnold greeted.

"Yes sir," Scottie addressed, as he knew it was him.

"Scottie, I am calling you because Abigail was in a bad accident, and we are here at General Regional Hospital. I thought you might want to be here. Please ask your parents to come with you," Mr. Arnold explained. Scottie's heart felt as if it was about to explode, and as if the air had completely left the room. He was unable to breathe- like someone had knocked all the air from his lungs. "Scottie, are you still there?" Mr. Arnold asked softly.

"Yes sir, I am here," he struggled to get the words out. "We will be right there."

"Please be careful," Mr. Arnold stated in his concerned voice.

"Yes sir." He said.

Scottie hung up and dropped the phone on his bed. He sat down on the side of the bed rubbing his now sweating palms on his pajama pants. *How could this happen? She is always careful, especially at night.* He placed his elbows on his knees and his face in his hands. *Oh my, please Abby, I cannot lose you.* He rubbed his face and slapped his hands on his legs. He stood up and started throwing on clothes.

Scottie entered the living room where his parents were talking. Mrs. Trudy was the first to see his face as he entered. "Scottie are you okay?" Mrs. Trudy asked.

"No ma'am, I am not," he answered. "Mr. Arnold just called me to inform that Abby was in a bad wreck, and said we should get to the hospital," he said with every restraint in him not to let his emotions show.

"Oh my!" Mrs. Trudy yelped as she jumped up from the sofa and grabbed her phone. She phoned their babysitter who lived a few houses over to come and stay with Stacy until they got back home. She rushed over and they left for the hospital.

When they arrived at the waiting room, the Whittingers were sitting together on a small two-chair sofa. Mrs. Trudy rushed over to where Mrs. Mia was sitting, she stood, and they embraced each other. You could see the love from a mother comforting the broken heart of another. Mr. Matthew walked over and shook Mr. Arnold's hand. "We got here as fast as we could," he stated with the other hand squeezing Mr. Arnold's shoulder. Scottie looked over and saw that the Johnson's were there also. He and Miranda made eye contact, and she leaped from her seat, ran, and hugged him.

"I hope she will be okay," Miranda said as she started to cry, with her head resting on his shoulder.

"Hey, don't forget our Abby is a fighter. She will be fine," he assured her. Meanwhile, he was battling the same emotions as Miranda in his mind, but he wanted to be strong for her. She was the only one whom he had ever confessed his feelings to about Abigail in the ninth grade. *That was so long ago. Surely, she doesn't remember it,* he thought to himself.

Mrs. Trudy and Mrs. Patsy greeted one another with a hug, and they all sat down next to each other. The men stood off in a circle murmuring that Mr. Arnold was telling them what had happened. Scottie stood close by to be able to eavesdrop on what they were saying.

"We got the call about 10:15 PM from the state trooper stating that Abigail was hit broadside by an 18-wheeler truck. The driver was tired from working a double shift and was drifting off to sleep when he ran through the red light. Abigail's car flipped several times before resting on the driver's side. First Responders had to use the Jaws of Life to cut her out of the car. She was then airlifted here. When we arrived, they told us that she was in surgery, and they would let us know as soon as they have her in stable condition." Mr. Arnold explained. They shook their heads in disbelief at the horrific accident Abigail had just been in.

"Was the driver of the truck hurt?" Mr. Thomas asked.

"Yes, he has some broken bones and cuts. They are working on him as well, although it is non-life threatening. He should pull through okay," Mr. Arnold explained. Scottie leaned against the wall. *Why did this happen to Abby? She doesn't deserve this. It should have been me instead. I would have driven right past the accident if I didn't have to take Amy home.* Scottie thought to himself. Miranda had taken a seat with her mom.

Scottie walked over and sat next to Mrs. Mia, though he could see she was in a worrisome state of mind, though she was holding it all together on the outside. That was Mrs. Mia, though no matter what she was going through, a hectic day, stressful moment, or something that would have anyone else in panic mode, she was always calm and collected. If I had to describe her, I would say she is a serene woman. Never a harsh word nor ever a frown have I seen on her face. Abigail was much like her mother, but she had her moments.

He looked at her with tear-filled eyes, “I am so sorry. I should've asked her to ride with us tonight, and this wouldn't have happened.”

Mrs. Mia wrapped her arm around Scottie and answered in her sweet soft voice, “Oh Scottie, you cannot blame yourself, things happen and there is no one to blame. This is just a small bump in our journey, though we don't know the purpose or outcome at this very moment. We have faith in God that He will get us through it.”

“How is she?” He asked as he turned to wipe away tears, hoping no one saw.

Mr. Arnold answered, “We were only told she was taken into surgery as soon as she had arrived. They told us that she was badly hurt. The nurse behind the counter said that they will let us know as soon as they know more.” Every concern of his was shown on his face. He was a very expressible, joyful man. He held nothing back about his emotions and when he did, his face would say it all. He is one of those people you see described in memes that though they say nothing their face tells it all. “I am going to get a cup of coffee. Would you like some?” He asked as he walked over, squatted, and placed his hand on Mrs. Mia’s should.

“No, thank you.” She replied.

“Would anyone care for coffee or anything?” He inquired.

“No sir,” Scottie replied. Everyone shook their heads. Mr. Arnold stood up and began to walk to the cafeteria.

“We will come with you,” Mr. Horman stated as he and Mr. Johnson followed suit behind him.

As they left the room Scottie placed his elbows on his knees with his face in his hands. He started going through the memories of his life with Abby. *What if I never get the chance to tell her my true feelings about her? What if she doesn't pull through? What if...* his cell started to ring and interrupted his thoughts. *Amy* read across his phone caller ID. *Oh no.* "Hello,"

"Are you really at the hospital without me?" Amy scorned. He glanced over at Mrs. Mia who heard the shrieking sound from his phone and looked over at him. "I will be right back," he stated while covering the mouthpiece of the phone.

"Who are you talking to? Scottie Horman, answer me!" she screamed even more.

Scottie walked down the hall from the waiting room. "Amy, calm down."

"Calm down? Calm down?" she hissed, "Don't tell me to calm down when you are at the hospital, and you didn't even bother to call me or come get me!"

"Amy, my parents and I came up here as soon as Abby's dad called," he snapped back. "There was no time to call, and I was too shaken up to drive."

"Really, why didn't you just call me? I would have come and picked you up."

"There was no time. I wanted to get here as fast as I could. She is in surgery at this moment, and we don't know how she is doing."

"ARE YOU SERIOUS SCOTTIE? You do have feelings for her, don't you?" She screamed.

"Look, if you aren't concerned about Abby, and all you want to do is fight then I am done talking to you. I don't have time for this right now." He snapped back.

"Fine, Bye!" Amy shouted as she hung up.

Scottie leaned against the wall. *Has she lost her mind? What is her deal? It is as if she isn't worried about Abby at all. Why do I put up with this?* "Ugh, there are more serious matters at hand. I can deal with her later," he mumbled to himself as he pushed himself from the wall and walked back to the waiting room.

As he entered the room, Miranda met him. “Is everything okay?” She asked.

“Yes, I am fine. Just Amy and her usual drama.” Scottie answered.

“Oh, I see,” she said with a slight smirk. “You want to talk about it?”

“Not really. I am just done with all of it. Now is not the time for her screaming matches, and self-centered attitude.” He stated.

“Well, I am here if you want to chat.” She said.

“Thank you. Let's sit and wait to hear from the doctor,” he suggested. She agreed and they went and took a seat across from their moms and Mrs. Mia.

“It is getting late, we need to get home to relieve the babysitter,” Mr. Matthew reminded Mrs. Trudy as they returned from the cafeteria.

“Oh dear, I didn't realize it was so late,” she said as she looked at her watch.

“We better get going too,” Mr. Thomas stated as he stood up from his seat. Scottie and Miranda insisted on staying until they heard how Abigail was doing.

“It is fine with us if it is okay with y'all,” Mr. Arnold said. They all agreed. The men shook hands and patted each other on the back. While the women squeezed each other tight.

“I will be back to check on you first thing in the morning,” Mrs. Trudy said.

“I will check on you later. Call me if you need me before then. No matter the time,” Mrs. Patsy insisted.

They spent the night in the waiting room when a doctor walked into the room. “Whittinger Family?” He asked as he gazed around the room with people sparsely spread out. They stood instantaneously as if it were rehearsed. He walked over to where they stood “Hello, I am Dr. Pete Robertson,” he said as he was massaging the rest of the hand sanitizer on his hands.

"How is she?" Mrs. Mia asked almost as if she was showing a moment of a bit of being impatient, which understandable giving the circumstance.

The doctor began to explain her injuries, "She has suffered serious injuries. She had some hemorrhaging due to some of the injuries that transpired in the wreck. Her face is swollen with bruising, and she has some minor scrapes as well. She is in an induced coma for her safety to help with the healing, at least till the brain swelling subsides. We had to put some stitches in a cut along her hairline. She had a collapsed lung, so we had to insert a tube into her side to assist her breathing. Her liver sustained severe trauma, and we are monitoring it very closely. Her left arm was broken in three places. We performed surgery, and it is in a cast. She is still in critical condition for the next 24 hours. I am sorry I cannot give you more information than that at this time."

Tears were streaming down Mr. and Mrs. Whittinger's faces. "Doctor, do you know how long she will be in the coma?" Mr. Arnold asked as if he was doing his best to hold back his emotions for Mrs. Mia.

"I am not certain. She is in recovery at this moment and will be taken to ICU once they have her room prepared for her. She will be monitored in the good care of our staff."

"May we see her?" Mrs. Mia asked as she lifted her head from Mr. Arnold's chest and wiped away her tears with a tissue.

"Yes, but please remember she is not going to look like the Abigail you saw last night before the trauma of the wreck. You may not even recognize her," he said as if trying to prepare them for the worst.

"Can she hear us when we speak to her?" Scottie asked.

Dr. Robertson looked at him with all compassion that you can expect in moments like this from medical staff, "It has not been medically proven if someone in the state of a coma can hear you, but I can tell you that it never hurts to talk to them as you normally do in your day-to-day contact. I will give y'all some time with her, but once she is moved to ICU you will have to follow their visitation hours."

"Thank you, Doctor," Mr. Arnold stated in heartfelt gratitude for his kindness and thoroughness of the situation at hand.

"You are welcome," he turned to a nurse standing at the counter and asked, "Sandy, can you kindly show the Whittingers to their daughter's recovery room?"

When they walked into the room, a nurse was checking Abigail's vitals. She was just as the doctor described "unrecognizable". She didn't even look like Abigail, who just 24 hours before was all smiles and giggles with her dirty, blonde, wavy hair bouncing in a ponytail. Her brown eyes were sparkling with joy. Her face now was swollen almost to the size of a soccer ball, and it looked as if someone had used it for a hacky sack. Her eyes were swollen shut, black and blue, and she had a bandage over her head, assuming that was to cover the area where the stitches were applied to her hairline. They had her on a ventilator to assist her breathing. Her left arm lay beside her in a white cast. Tubes and wires were running out from under her hospital gown to all the machines.

"Is she in pain?" Mrs. Mia asked as she took hold of her bruised right arm, which had her IV line in it to provide her with liquids and medicine.

The nurse looked over the blood pressure monitor she had just read. "No ma'am," she answered in a soft voice. She was a petite young lady. She looked like she was still in high school though she was around 24 or so years old. She had her shoulder-length, blonde hair pulled up in a messy bun. Her green eyes were almost the color of the Caribbean Sea. "We have given her some morphine to help keep her pain to the bare minimum if any at all," she explained. As she walked around the bed to exit the room, she spoke to them softly, "If you need anything, push the nurse's button."

“Thank you.” Mrs. Mia said as she sat in the chair that Mr. Arnold had pulled up for her next to the bed. Scottie and Miranda stood on the other side of the bed. Tears ran down their faces. It was hard to see her like this. In just a moment, their lives had been slammed with a tragedy that could have been much worse.

“We are here, Abigail.” Mrs. Mia spoke in a soft tone. She looked up at Mr. Arnold who was standing behind her. “Please say a prayer,” she asked. He nodded, and they all took one another’s hand and bowed their heads as he began to pray. Peace came over the room as Mr. Arnold finished the prayer.

“She is going to be just fine,” Mr. Arnold assured her with a smile and squeezed her shoulder. She patted his hand and nodded in agreement.

“It felt like you were just born yesterday. Your father and I were relaxing on the couch watching a movie and eating pizza. We started taking our nights rather easy after I reached my 38th week of pregnancy. I would lay back on the couch and your dad massaged my feet during the movie. As I think of it, I have not had a foot massage since.” She giggled and looked up at Mr. Arnold, seeing a tear stream down his cheek. He chuckled and wiped the tear away. She turned back her glance to Abigail. “I was in my 40th week, and I started having contractions early that morning. They had been off and, on all day, but I just took them as more Braxton hicks. We were about mid of the movie when my water broke. It was a bit funny at first because I thought you had kicked my bladder and caused me to have an accident.” She giggled. “We arrived at the hospital, and we thought you would arrive quickly, but it was quite the opposite. Once I received the epidural it seemed to come to a screeching halt. You decided to wait and make your appearance the next morning at 8:15 AM.” A tear strolled down her face as she continued, “I remember hearing your first cry, and in that one moment, I was overwhelmed with so much joy and love that I started to cry with you. When the nurse placed you in my arms and I held you for the first time my heart was almost bursting with every beat." Tears flowed down her face as she gripped Abigail's hand.

Mr. Arnold stated he remembered the first time he held her. "My heart was full of so much pride. I was now a Daddy to a beautiful little girl," Mr. Arnold spoke softly, "you opened your eyes and looked up at me and my heart skipped a beat. My life was never the same when you wrapped your little hand around my finger, because I knew then and there that you had me wrapped around your finger," he said with a smile. "I made a vow then that I would do anything in this world for you to be happy and to keep you safe." A tear streamed down his face as he placed his hand lightly on Abigail's head.

They sat in silence listening to the monitors, and her breathing. Everyone flashed back to their moments with her. When a nurse walked in, "I am sorry, but y'all will need to leave now. We are moving her to a room on the ICU floor. Our visiting hours start at 6:30 in the morning and y'all can come back then. We will call you if there are any updates or changes before then."

Mr. Arnold looked at his watch, "It is 4:15 AM. We can go home, get a shower and a bite to eat, and return then." He looked at Mrs. Mia. She nodded in agreement. She stood and leaned over the bed and kissed Abigail on her forehead.

"Please fight my darling. Fight with all your might. We will be back soon." Mr. Arnold guided her to the door.

Miranda stood up next to the bed. "You are more like a sister to me than a best friend, and I need you to be okay. I need you to get better. We are supposed to be starting college soon, and I am not going to go alone. You hear me. I love you, Abigail." She rubbed her left arm and walked out of the room.

Scottie came close to her side, leaned over and whispered soft and low in her ear. "Please get better, Abby. I don't want to know what my life would be like without you in it. I am here for you, always have, and always will." He placed a soft kiss on her forehead. They all took one last look at her before leaving her for the night.

# CHAPTER 12

## Everyone Knows

*It has been eight days since the accident, and she is still in a medically induced coma.* Scottie thought to himself as he lay in bed. It was Sunday morning, and he decided to get some rest first and be there for visiting hours at 8:00 AM instead of 6:00 AM. He hadn't rested much since the accident. He turned to check the time on the clock, *6:45 PM, I better get up and get dressed.* The what-ifs returned as he combed his hair. *What if there is more damage than the doctors realize? What if she is not able to wake up from the coma? What if she is paralyzed?* "Ugh," he shook his head as if erasing a sketch board. "I have got to stop thinking like this. I know Abby, she is a fighter, and we will overcome this."

"WE!?" Mrs. Trudy interrupted. Scottie jolted and turned to the door.

"Yes, WE! I have never left her to battle any situation alone, and I am surely not starting now," he replied as he sat on the bed to put on his shoes. She sat down next to him on the bed.

"Son, if you ever need to talk, I am here. I know you are having a tough time with Abigail's accident, and I don't want to pressure you. Just know that I am here."

"Mom, what if when she wakes up she isn't the same Abby?" He asked.

"Let's not focus on all the 'what ifs'. As you said, Abigail is a fighter, and when she does wake up you will be there for her as you always have been," she encouraged as she put her arm around him. "Although there are some decisions that you need to make sooner or later."

"Decisions?" he asked, not having any idea where this was coming from.

"I have noticed that you and Amy have been at odds here lately. Well, more than your norm I should say," she chuckled, trying to lighten his spirits.

"Okay?" He said.

"Everyone sees your true feelings and knows that she isn't the one you long to be with, but we just don't understand why you torture yourself and fight back those emotions. Your dad and I want you to be happy, and not be with someone who makes you miserable. You walk around with guilt loading you down when we truly believe you don't have to. Just take some time away from Amy. I am not saying you must break up with her. I am just asking you to take some time to figure things out for yourself. I just want you to be happy and I can see you are nowhere near happy. Abigail needs you right now more than ever, and when she wakes up, she will need you even more. To be there for her you must be in the right state of mind, and at this moment you are swarmed with emotions. It seems that you are having issues trying to cope with them. I am always here for you to help you in any way I can, but I cannot make any decisions for you. I can only listen and guide you through them. I know I have said more than I needed to already, so I am going to leave you to finish what you were doing. Let me know when you are leaving. I will be making some breakfast if you have time to eat."

She pat him on the back and stood to leave. "Mom," he called out before she reached the door.

"Yes?" She turned to face him.

"Thank you. I didn't know that anyone knew. I have had these feelings bottled up for so long, and you are right I need to fix myself before I can even begin to be there for her." He explained.

"You are welcome, that is what moms are for," she winked and walked out the door.

Scottie threw himself back on the bed. "Everyone knows!?" he said out loud to himself wondering how that is even possible since he hasn't told anyone except Miranda in the ninth grade. *Surely not everyone. How will I even begin to explain this to Amy?* He looked over at the clock, 7:15 AM. "Well, she will have to wait." He got up and grabbed his wallet and keys from his dresser. He walked downstairs and told his mom goodbye.

Scottie arrived at the hospital. He still had ten minutes before they could allow visitors into the ICU, so he went into the cafeteria to grab a quick morning snack. As he entered, he saw Mr. Arnold in line for coffee. He walked over to stand beside him in line.

"Good morning," he said as he sneaked up beside him. Mr. Arnold turned to him and said, "Good morning, Scottie."

"Any news?" he asked as he grabbed an orange juice from the cooler. Mr. Arnold shook his head. "They say her vitals are stable, and she is healing at the expected rate. She is out of the woods. So if everything continues going in this direction, they can take her out of the medically induced coma soon. They just want to monitor for a few more days to make certain."

"That is great news!" Scottie said with excitement. He grabbed a banana and a bowl of oatmeal from the breakfast bar, paid the cashier, and took his seat at a table next to Mr. Arnold.

"I appreciate you for coming here every day, Scottie. She is so blessed to have friends like you and Miranda." Mr. Arnold said.

"If you ask me, I am the one who is blessed to have her in my life. She kept my head on straight. I don't know where I would be without her." Scottie stated.

"She was so scared of leaving her friends in San Antonio to move here, but y'all welcomed her with such kindness that made her transition easier. Y'all have been almost inseparable since. I could not have picked better friends for her myself." Mr. Arnold added.

"You are welcome. Abby is just one of those girls that you can be comfortable around. Now I can't imagine my life without her in it," Scottie paused thinking about the words that just came out of his mouth. *Oh my, did I just admit to Abby's dad that I can't live without her in my life? Will he see through to my true feelings?*

Mr. Arnold placed his hand on Scottie's shoulder. "It's okay, Scottie. I know how much you care for her. Like I said earlier, she is out of the woods and doing much better. Y'all will be going off to college in no time." Scottie shook his head and blinked to keep the tears from his eyes. He started to eat his oatmeal. Mr. Arnold removed his hand and began eating his breakfast. They sat quietly eating their breakfast as if they were both lost in their thoughts.

It was time for visitation. They gathered their items off the table and threw them in the trash on their way out of the cafeteria. As they were getting into the elevator, Scottie's phone rang and "Amy" appeared on the ID. He silenced the call and slid it back into his pocket. Within moments, it was ringing again. He pulled it out of his pocket and saw it was Amy once more. He put it on vibrate only.

"Are you sure you don't need to answer that?" Mr. Arnold asked.

"No sir. She can wait." He placed the phone back in his pocket.

The elevator doors opened, and they entered the ICU floor. You could hear the beeping of the machines, and some ventilators breathing for the patients. It put a sickening feeling in Scottie's stomach. He knew that if it was this hard for him, he could not imagine how her parents were feeling. Mrs. Mia was already in the room with Abigail when they arrived at her doorway. Scottie excused himself to the waiting room and gave them privacy. They would only allow two people to be in her room at once. Scottie made his way down the hall to the ICU waiting room. When he opened the door, he spotted Miranda sitting by the window. She seemed lost in her thoughts staring out the window. There wasn't much of a view. From the window, you could see the lower floor roof, and past that, it looked over other lower buildings that surrounded the hospital.

Scottie took the seat next to her, "how are you?"

"As to be expected I guess," Miranda answered, turning to face him. "You know I still can't believe this is all real. I feel like I am stuck in a nightmare and cannot wake up."

"I understand. I was thinking on the way here that I can't even imagine how her parents are coping with all this." Scottie agreed.

"You are right." She leaned her head against the window.

"Mr. Arnold thanked me for us being so kind and accepting of her when they moved here. As I thought about it, it just seems like yesterday that I met her." He continued.

Miranda nodded her head, "yeah, it does."

Scottie's phone was vibrating in his pocket. He pulled it out and saw it was Amy calling again. *Why is she blowing up my phone? She knows I come to the hospital every morning. Why would today be any different?* He placed the phone in his back pocket.

"Is that Amy?" Miranda inquired.

"Yes. She is blowing up my phone this morning." He leaned back in his chair.

"Maybe she is scared to leave you alone for too long with Abigail." She said.

"Why would she be scared of that?" he asked, placing his elbow on the chair between them. Shocked by Miranda's suggestion.

"Scottie, sooner or later you are going to have to face reality." She stated.

"Reality?" He inquired.

"We all know, and I am almost 99.9% sure Amy knows as well. She is just hoping that once she gets you out of Savannah, and alone with her, then you will forget all about Abigail." Miranda stated the obvious.

"You all know what? And why would I ever forget about Abby? She is my..." he continued.

"Don't say friend, Scottie!" Miranda interrupted. "I am sick of these games y'all have been playing for years. It has gone on long enough. If you want to be with Amy then be with her, but if you want to be with Abigail then for heaven's sake break up with Amy and let her move on."

Scottie sat in silence. The way he did not deny that he had feelings for Abigail proved to her that she was right all along.

"I am sorry, Scottie. I don't mean to come off as cruel, but as we live in this very moment, sitting in this waiting room, it is teaching us that life is too short!" Miranda stood up from her chair. "Please tell them I will see her at the next visitation. I have an appointment that I can't be late for." She grabbed her things.

"Miranda," Scottie whispered as she placed her purse on her shoulder and turned to look at him. "Does everyone really know?"

"Yes. It has been obvious for years. You two were the only ones too blind to see it. Call me if there are any changes." Scottie nodded and Miranda left the waiting room. It was total silence in the waiting room.

"Where is Miranda?" Mrs. Mia asked when she and Mr. Arnold walked into the room.

"She said she was sorry, but she had an appointment she had to get to. She will be back for the evening visit."

Mr. Arnold sat down next to Scottie, "you can go see her now. Take your time. We will be here waiting for you when you get out."

Scottie entered her room. It was hard to see her with all the tubes and wires running everywhere. The bruising on her face faded away with each passing day. Her scars were healing well from the cuts that made gashes in her skin. He pulled up the chair next to her bed and sat down close to her. *Everyone knows* he could hear Miranda as if she was sitting in the room with him. He took Abigail's free hand in his. "Abby, do you know how I feel about you? I should have told you a long time ago. I remember the day you walked into my life, and I cannot see you walking out of it. I want to be more than just your friend. I have been so scared to tell you all these years in fear that you don't feel the same. I believe Miranda was hinting that you feel the same, but you have made it clear that I am nothing more than a big brother. I don't want things to go back to the way they were. I am going to break up with Amy and give us a chance. No matter what you must face when you come out of your coma, I am here Abby. I always have and always will."

*What Ifs – Kane Brown (feat. Lauren Alaina)*

# CHAPTER 13

## What If

It has been twelve days since they placed Abigail in a medically induced coma. Scottie was hoping today will be the day they will decide to bring her out of it. At least they have her in a room now and they can visit whenever they want, but everyone likes to be there early for the doctor's morning route for his patients. He pulled into the hospital parking lot, and parked in the first available spot. He turned off the engine and sat for a moment. *What if she does wake up, will she have any issues? How can I tell her how I feel about her? What if she doesn't feel the same?* "Enough of the what-ifs, just go in already!" He told himself and got out of the car.

Abigail's parents and Miranda were sitting around her bed speaking in low voices as if they may wake her up. "Good morning, any news?" he asked as he took the empty seat by Miranda.

"The doctor hasn't made his round just yet," Mr. Arnold answered. "Shouldn't be too long now."

"I am hoping we get good news today," Mrs. Mia said. "Her scars are healing nicely, and her complexion has come back, which gives me faith that she will be just fine."

"I agree," Miranda assured.

Everyone sat for a few moments looking at her fragile body lying in bed. She looked as if she was only sleeping and would soon wake up to greet them all. *Only one could hope,* Scottie thought. A knock on the door brought him back to the room.

"Hello," Dr. Robertson greeted. He had on his pristine, white doctor's coat, with the stethoscope around his neck, and navy-blue scrubs. Dark circles were under his green eyes showing a lack of sleep. "How is our girl doing today?" He opened her chart and began reading over it. He closed the chart and looked at her vitals on the machines.

"She looks even better today," Mrs. Mia asserted as she watched him place his pen in his pocket.

"Yes. Everything looks good, with her vitals as well. The hole from her chest tube is healing up quickly. She will have a small scar on her side, but it won't be very noticeable. We still have some concerns." He turned and rested his hands on the rail of her bed. "But I believe we are out of danger for any bleeding on the brain, and it seems she can breathe on her own now. I am going to take her out of the medically induced coma." Everyone in the room gasped with excitement. He raised his hand as if to quiet a classroom full of excited children. "I am not going to tell you that all will be well, and she will be the same girl when she does wake up. It will take her some time to wake up. I just want you to prepare yourselves for the chance that she isn't the same," Dr. Robertson cautioned. Mrs. Mia knew the warnings that he was giving. She had heard him say that to other parents and family members that were in her spot on many shifts.

"Is that what you are expecting, doctor?" Miranda asked.

"I just don't want to give false hope. On the outside, Abigail is healing quickly, but the inside takes a longer process. Let's just wake her up and see where we are at then." He explained.

"That sounds great," Mr. Arnold praised. "I know my girl and she is a fighter. We will overcome whatever obstacles lie ahead." He stood and shook the doctor's hand.

"I can attest to that. She survived a horrific accident, and is still here to tell everyone about it," Dr. Robertson proclaimed. "She is blessed to have y'all as her support group. Stay as long as you like, and we will keep watch on her as we stop feeding the medicine in her IV. It may take some hours for her to come out of the coma, so be patient."

"Thank you," Mrs. Mia emphasized as he opened the door to leave.

"You are welcome. I am only a call away." He shut the door behind him.

Everyone beamed with excitement. It was the news they had been waiting days to hear.

"I am going to call my parents," Scottie announced.

"Me too," Miranda stood up and joined him.

Mr. Arnold and Mrs. Mia hugged each other with excitement. "I am going to go call everyone to let them know the news," Mrs. Mia gasped.

"Good idea. I will step out to call work and let everyone know." He left the room as if he was on cloud nine.

Mrs. Mia kept her fears to herself and took the alone time to pray. She asked the Lord to continue to keep his hand on Abigail, and that she would wake up with minimum to no serious conditions. If it is not your will, please give us the knowledge and strength to get us through it. She ended her prayer thanking Him for the healing He had done and will do in her life.

They all sat in Abigail's room and told stories of their times with her. Their laughter was carried out into the hall. It was a much happier sound than it had been in the past week, or so. Time had zoomed by them, and it was now noon. "Oh my, it is lunchtime," Mr. Arnold said when he looked down at his watch. "Would y'all like to go grab a bite to eat?"

"I don't want to leave her alone just in case she does wake up," Mrs. Mia said.

"If you would like, y'all can go grab a bite in the cafeteria. Miranda and I can stay here with her. If she does wake up, we can call you," Scottie suggested.

Miranda nodded, "I don't mind staying. I am not that hungry right now."

"Are you sure? Y'all don't mind?" Mrs. Mia questioned.

"Not at all," Scottie assured.

"We will be downstairs if anything does change dear. We won't go far," Mr. Arnold assured. She nodded in agreement. "Would y'all like for us to bring you anything back?" They both shook their heads no. "We won't be long." They said and left.

Mr. Arnold and Mrs. Mia left the room and headed down to the cafeteria. "I feel so sorry for them," Miranda said as she adjusted to get comfortable in her chair.

"Yeah. I feel so helpless. I wish there was more I could do." Scottie agreed.

"So, we haven't been able to talk lately. How have you been holding up?" Miranda asked.

"I am good. I am thankful for the good news today." He stated.

"I agree!" Miranda said with a joyous tone. "How has Amy been taking it with you coming up here to visit?"

"Well, it isn't any of her business anymore." He replied.

"It never was really, but I don't follow you. Are y'all not together anymore?" She inquired.

"Nope. I broke up with her after you and I talked in the waiting room that day." Scottie answered, playing with a loose thread on the hem of his jeans.

"WHAT? What took you so long?" Miranda asked.

"It was her attitude and constant bickering with me after Abby's wreck. I just couldn't take it anymore, so I called it off." He explained.

"I am sure she didn't take it well." She added.

"Not at all. She said she knew I had been hiding my feelings for Abigail throughout our entire relationship, and that I had strung her along for all these years. She had a few more choice words before she hung up on me. I haven't spoken to her since." He continued.

"I am so glad you finally opened your eyes and saw the light." Miranda chuckled.

"I am just glad that I don't have to put up with her drama and demands anymore. It has been a whole lot more peaceful. That is for sure." He added.

"I can imagine so. So, when she wakes up are you going to tell her?" She asked.

"I have been giving it some thought. I really would like to see where she stands with that. I don't want to tell her anything and then she doesn't feel the same. It will make things awkward and that is the last thing I want. I would rather prefer that she is happy with someone else as long as I can remain in her life. I can live with that. It is her not being in my life at all that I cannot live with." He stated.

"I am almost positive she feels the same way as you do. She is just as stubborn as you, so she may not confess her feelings either," Miranda stated. "You two have always avoided the obvious."

"I just know that since her accident things have not been the same. I cannot speak for the past. Just keep thinking about the what ifs." He said.

"What ifs?" Miranda asked.

"Yeah, you know. What if I had driven her home? What if I had left the bowling alley before her? What if I had told her at prom? What if she doesn't feel the same after I tell her and doesn't want to be friends anymore? What if she doesn't fully recover?" He went on and on.

"That is torture, Scottie. You need to stop that kind of thinking right now!" Miranda insisted. "There is nothing you could have done to prevent what happened that night, just like any of us. I don't know why this happened, but I do know it is out of our hands. You don't know what the future holds for you and Abigail, but torturing yourself with all the questions of what-ifs is not good, and you need to stop. If you want to dwell on the what-ifs, dwell on the positive ones. What if she is the same Abigail that we have been friends with since freshman year? What if she does feel the same, and you two last throughout eternity? That is what you need to dwell on and stop beating yourself up. It is not worth it, nor is it doing you or Abigail any good."

"Sorry we took so long," Mr. Arnold stated as they walked in the door.

"Oh, y'all are fine. No changes to her condition." Miranda stated. Scottie leaned back in his chair and forced a smile on his face.

"It has been hours now. Hopefully, she will start to wake up soon," Mrs. Mia said as she sat in her seat next to the bed. "We have never been through this situation before, but surely it won't take much longer for her to wake up."

"We will stay here as long as it takes," Mr. Arnold assured. Miranda and Scottie went down to the cafeteria to grab something to eat and was back in the room within an hour.

They sat, telling stories of their moments with Abigail. "Do you remember the time that Amy found out that Scottie and Abigail had danced together?" Miranda asked.

"Do I ever. I heard about that for months," Scottie smirked.

"Well, I would like to hear this story," Mr. Arnold insisted.

"Well, it was one summer night. It couldn't have been more than two summers ago. Scottie and his parents had gone out with us downtown for dinner at Vannie's Van Gogo's pizza. We were sitting outside on the patio. The weather was nice with a slight breeze. There was a live band playing on the balcony at the Tree House Savannah. We all enjoyed the night dancing and visiting with one another. What we weren't aware of was that Mari-Kate had come in to pick up a pizza to go and saw Scottie and Abigail dancing together. Of course, nothing else happened," Miranda assured.

"You couldn't make Amy ever believe that" Scottie said.

"I can only imagine," Mrs. Mia giggled. "I remember Abigail telling me the story."

"We still can't believe that you have not kicked her to the curb," Mr. Arnold stated.

"Arnold!" Mrs. Mia said abruptly.

"It's ok, Mrs. Mia. He has a point, but just to let y'all know, I have broken up with Amy." Scottie cut in.

They both looked intrigued. "Scottie, you don't have to share your personal life with us," Mrs. Mia said.

"It's ok. I just couldn't deal with her after the accident. She was always complaining about how much time I spent up here, and then if I was with her, I was only there in body. Plus, I think it is the right thing to do with her starting college soon." Scottie explained.

"What about you? Aren't you going to the same college?" Miranda asked.

"I have withdrawn my application, and placed everything on hold until we find out how Abby is doing," Scottie answered.

Mr. Arnold leaned toward Scottie, "Scottie, you cannot place your life on hold. You need to go to college. Abigail would not want that," he said in a soft tone.

Mrs. Mia and Miranda agreed. "He is right, Scottie. She would not want you to do this," Mrs. Mia stated.

"Once I know she is okay and doing well, then I will transfer my application to a local college. I surely don't want to go anywhere far away from her." He was shocked that he spoke those words out loud in front of her parents.

"You have always been there for her, and I can never thank you enough. But you cannot stop your life for her. She would not want that. I am certain she would want you to better yourself with a deeper education so that you can pursue and succeed in your career," Mr. Arnold stated.

"He is right," Mrs. Mia agreed.

"I would just rather wait until she wakes up, and I know she is well again." Scottie added.

"Well don't delay it too long, because it will be easier to put off," Miranda said.

"I won't. I just want to wait until I know she is okay. Once I know that I will start looking into colleges." He assured them.

The room fell silent for a while. Everyone was lost in their thoughts. When Mrs. Mia noticed Abigail's hand moving. She looked up to see Abigail blinking.

"Abigail!" She jumped with excitement and leaned over so she could see her. Everyone in the room gasped.

"Go get the nurse," Mr. Arnold shrieked. Scottie shot out the door and ran down the hall.

Mr. Arnold ran around to the other side of the bed to get into Abigail's view. Tears started flowing down everyone's faces. Abigail looked frightened. "It's okay. You were in an accident, and you are in the hospital. Scottie has gone to get the nurse." Mrs. Mia explained. Abigail squeezed her hand.

The nurse, Carrie, entered the room. "Step back everyone, let me look at her." She instructed as she came to Mr. Arnold's side of the bed. "Everyone please step outside while I assist Carrie," Nurse Susan stated. "We will take good care of her. We know y'all are excited to see her awake. We need to make sure her vitals are good and that she is capable of breathing on her own. Once we get her settled, we will let y'all come back in." she reassured them as she ushered them out into the hallway.

After what seemed like forever to them in the hallway, Carrie opened the door to let them back in. The nurses had now taken the ventilator out and slightly raised the head of Abigail's bed so that she wasn't lying flat on her back anymore. Mrs. Mia rushed to her bedside and leaned over to hug her, and Mr. Arnold joined in on the opposite side. Scottie and Miranda stood silently at the end of her bed. "You gave us quite a scare," Mr. Arnold stated as he took his seat next to the bed. Abigail's smile made Scottie's heart skip a few beats. It had been so long since that smile warmed up his darkest days. She pointed at her throat, and in a whisper asked for some water. Miranda poured her some ice water from the small container the nurses had filled with ice that morning. She handed the water to Abigail. She took a few sips and smiled.

"That helped," she said in a low tone. The ventilator had aggravated her throat after being in a coma, so it made it hard for her to speak loudly. "What happened? How long have I been here?" she asked.

"You were on your way home from the bowling alley and a big truck ran the red light. You have been in a coma to allow your inner parts to heal," Mrs. Mia explained.

"How long have I been here?" She muttered.

"A little over a week," Miranda answered.

Abigail looked in shock, "I have been in a coma for a week?"

Mrs. Mia shook her head. "We have all been here as soon as the visiting doors were opened and grasped every minute we could before heading back home. We all have been very worried about you," Mrs. Mia said.

"I knew you were going to be okay. You are stubborn and a fighter," Scottie said softly, holding onto the end of the bed. He smirked at her hoping to receive that beautiful smile once more. Except she didn't smile, she just looked at him with a puzzled look.

"Do I know you?" Abigail asked. Everyone looked at each other in shock. "I am sorry if I said something wrong."

"You don't know who he is," Mr. Arnold said. Abigail shook her head. Scottie's chest began to grow tight, and it felt as if he could not breathe. "Do you know everyone else in the room?" She shook her head no once more. "Who do you not know?" She lifted her finger and pointed to Miranda and Scottie. Miranda gasped. Mrs. Mia placed her arms around her to comfort her. Scottie turned and walked out of the room. Mr. Arnold pressed the nurse call button.

"Yes, can I help you?" Nurse Carrie answered.

"Yes, we need someone to come see, please." Mr. Arnold answered.

Nurse Carrie entered the room, "How can I be of assistance? Do you need to be raised some more?" She asked as she went to the head of the bed.

"No," Mrs. Mia answered. "I am afraid something is wrong," she whispered.

"We have called the doctor and let him know Abigail is awake. He is headed up here now. What seems to be the problem?"

"Abigail doesn't remember us," Miranda's voice cracked as she uttered words that were so hard for her to say.

"She doesn't remember any of you?" The nurse asked.

"She knows us, but she doesn't know who her friends are," Mrs. Mia said consoling Miranda who was holding back tears in fear of frightening Abigail.

"I am going to go to the waiting room with Scottie. That way it won't put any stress on her. Please let us know what the doctor's findings are," Miranda stated.

Mrs. Mia nodded in agreement, "of course."

Miranda looked to Abigail who looked so confused over what was taking place. "I hope you get to go home soon, and I am glad to know you are going to be okay." Miranda left the room to find Scottie. She pulled her phone out of her pocket and dialed his number. "Scottie, where are you?"

"I had to get out of there. I couldn't breathe." Scottie said.

"Where are you," Miranda asked once more.

"I am in the waiting room. I wanted to wait to see what the doctor says." He replied.

"Stay there. I am on my way," Miranda interrupted.

When she arrived in the waiting room, she saw Scottie in a chair with his elbows resting on his knees and his face covered with his hands. She went and sat down in the empty seat next to him. She placed her hand on his back.

"Of all things I thought would happen, this was not one of them," he stated as he leaned back in the chair.

"I know what you mean." Miranda agreed.

"What if I have lost her? What if I never get the chance to love her like I have always wanted to? What if I wasted all these years with the wrong girl? What if…"

"That is enough, Scottie," Miranda insisted. "We cannot think like that. Maybe her brain is still trying to process everything, and it is just going to take a little longer than we may have expected."

"What if she doesn't get her memory back?" He continued.

"Then we will cross that bridge when we come to it, but we don't need to dwell on negative thoughts. "We will get through whatever comes our way together," she assured him. "I am going to call everyone to let them know she is awake. Will you be okay by yourself?" Scottie nodded his head and watched as she left the room. *How can she not remember me? What if she doesn't regain her memory? What would I do without her in my life?*

"Scottie," Mr. Arnold said as he placed his hands on Scottie's back. "Are you okay?"

"Yes sir. How is Abby?" Scotties asked.

"She is a little shaken up with all that has happened, but she is going to be fine. The doctor came in and looked her over. He suspects she just has a case of amnesia, but he is going to run more tests to make sure nothing serious is going on." He stated as he sat down.

"Did he have any suggestions as to what we can do to help her gain her memory? Or if she will recover her memory?" Scottie pressed on.

“He said there are therapists who can help people regain their memory. He let us know that it could take anywhere from days to maybe even years to regain her memory.” Mr. Arnold answered.

“Years!” Scottie gasped.

“Just give her some time. I am sure she will pull through this, especially with y’all by her side.” Mr. Arnold added.

“I am not going anywhere. I will do whatever I need to do to help her recover.” Scottie stated.

‘‘I know you will,” Mr. Arnold said.

# CHAPTER 14

## I Have My Best Friend Back

It had been three weeks since Abigail arrived home from the hospital. She had started her physical therapy sessions for her arm and saw a therapist to help with her memory loss. She was experiencing flashes of memory, but not enough to make sense of them.

"Abigail," Mrs. Mia called from the patio.

"Ma'am," Abigail answered. She marked her page with a bookmark and turned to where Mrs. Mia was standing in the doorway.

"Oh, there you are," she stated, walking toward her.

"Yes, ma'am. I thought it was a nice warm day to come lay by the pool to read," she answered, laying the book in her lap.

"I agree it is nice today," Mrs. Mia agreed. "I was heading to work and wanted to check on you before I go. Your dad had to go to the office to work on a case. We have our phones if you need anything. I left the Harmon's and Johnson's numbers on the fridge in case of emergency, and we are out of reach. I prepared chicken spaghetti in a pan for supper, it's in the freezer. Just follow the instructions taped to the top of the dish and you should be fine. I made a salad and placed it in the fridge for a side. Is there anything I can get you before I go?"

"No, ma'am," I should be good. I still have one good hand to use," she answered, raising her right arm.

"I can always call in if you aren't comfortable with being home alone yet," Mrs. Mia said.

"Mom, stop worrying. I will be just fine." She said.

"That is hard for a mom to do. You have only been home a few weeks, and I have mixed emotions about going back to work so soon." Mrs. Mia stated.

"I will be fine. I have my phone right here and will call if I need anything." She assured.

"Okay. I guess I better get going then. I love you," Mrs. Mia leaned over and kissed her forehead, and squeezed her tight as if it may be her last hug ever.

"Mom, I will be fine I promise," she said softly to reassure her.

"Okay. Don't hesitate to call," Mrs. Mia said as she reached the back door.

"I won't." She answered.

She watched as Mrs. Mia entered the house and closed the door behind her. Once she was out of sight, Abigail opened her book to the marked page and began to read it once again.

She was so immersed in her book that she didn't even realize it was almost six o'clock PM. She finished her chapter and placed her bookmark between the pages. She went inside to start dinner by following the instructions. She poured herself a glass of sweet, iced tea and sat down on the island to wait for the oven to preheat. The binder of photos, used in her therapy sessions, caught her attention at the end of the island. She pulled it to her and flipped through the different photos. "Why can't I remember?" Abigail said out loud. She looked at a photo of herself and a group of others. She turned the page, and a photo caught her eye. It was her and the guy from her hospital room sitting in a red convertible car, but it was in a building. With a description under it: Sock Hop, Sophomore year. Scottie and I. Beside that photo was her and the girl from the hospital in the same car. The description underneath read: Sock Hop, Sophomore year. Miranda and I. She glanced back and forth between the two photos. *We look like we had fun together,* Abigail thought to herself. The alarm on the oven beeped to notify it was preheated. Abigail stood and placed the dish in the oven and set the timer to one hour. She sat down and a flash of her and Miranda laughing in the pool went through her mind. *I wonder if she would come over and tell me stories about these photos,* she thought. "It doesn't hurt to ask," she told herself. She picked up her cell and scrolled through her contacts till she read MIRANDA, MY BFF. She contemplated for a moment on making the call. She pressed the name to call her, and the line began to ring. Then she heard a soft hello. Abigail didn't quite think through the call of what to say before calling. There was a slight pause.

"Abigail is that you?" Miranda asked.

"Yes, it is me," she answered. "I hope I am not bothering you."

"No, not at all. Are you okay?" Miranda said.

"Yes, I am fine. I am home alone, and I was going through the binder of photos that we have been using in my therapy sessions, and…." Abigail paused.

"Did you remember something?" Miranda asked.

"No, not really..." she paused again. "I had a flash of memory of us in the pool laughing."

"Oh, that's amazing!" Miranda exclaimed.

"I was thinking that if you don't mind. Could you come over and look at the binder with me? Maybe even share some stories about…." Abigail added.

"I would love to!" Miranda cut in.

"Really?" She asked

"Of course! I can be there in ten minutes. Is that okay?" Miranda stated.

"Sounds great. I will see you then," Abigail said. "Thank you."

"Any time. See you soon." Miranda replied.

"Bye," Miranda said and ended the call.

Abigail felt some excitement "Maybe this will be just what I need to help my memory."

Abigail was sitting on the sofa when Miranda arrived. “I thought it would be more comfortable on the sofa than sitting at the island. I can still hear the timer when it beeps for me to take the dinner out of the stove,” Abigail said as she led Miranda to the sofa in the living room.

“Sounds good to me,” Miranda said. “It’s hard to believe it has been so long since I have been here. I am glad you invited me over.”

“I was nervous at first. I didn’t know if you would want to come or not. Since we haven’t spoken since I awoke from the coma.”

“Of course, I would want to come. I have called and checked on you every day,” Miranda said as she sat down on the sofa.

“You have?” Abigail asked.

“Yes, I talk with your mom about how your therapy and physical therapy sessions are going. To see how you are doing.” Miranda answered.

“Oh, I had no idea.” Abigail said.

“We didn’t want to place any pressure on you while you are recovering, but I am glad to see that our photo binder came in handy,” Miranda said. She picked up the binder and started looking through the photos.

“You helped put this together?” Abigail asked.

“You and I put this together. It is a keepsake of us through the years. This is a photo of the three of us together,” Miranda explained. She pointed to a photo of her, Abigail, and Scottie. The description read: OUR FIRST LABOR DAY WEEKEND.

“My therapist and I go over these photos in the sessions hoping it will help my memory return. My mom told me that we have all been best friends since we moved here from San Antonio,” Abigail said as she moved closer to Miranda to view the album with her.

“Do you remember living in San Antonio?” Miranda asked.

"Yes, it is funny because that is the only thing I remember. I don't remember moving here." Abigail replied.

"Have you talked to any of your friends since the accident?" Miranda inquired.

"Yes, Isabella and I just face timed each other a few days ago," Abigail answered. "She called when she heard I was in an accident."

"Well, it is good that you have had someone to talk to." Miranda said.

"Yes, but I want to get back to my life here. I feel strange living in an environment I don't remember. That is why I asked you over. As I said on the phone, I have flashes of moments, but I can't put them all together. I thought that maybe if you told me stories it might help me to put two and two together." Abigail added.

"I would love to. Anything that will help. I have missed spending time with you. I have felt so lost. Not able to pick up the phone to call you or come over and stay. I missed having my best friend to confide in with things that I normally would." Miranda stated.

"My mom said we were inseparable," Abigail stated with a smile.

"We were," Miranda said. "So where would you like to begin?"

*Photograph – Ed Sheeran*

# CHAPTER 15

## I Wish I Could Remember

The girls spent the night talking over the photos. Miranda told Abigail stories of different times they shared. Mr. Arnold called to check on Abigail and was excited to hear that she invited Miranda over. He let her know that he shouldn't be home later than nine o'clock PM, and for them to call if they needed anything.

"So, is there anything, in particular, you would like to hear about?" Miranda asked.

"Now that you ask. I would like for you to tell me about this night," Abigail stated, pointing to the Sock Hop photo of her and Scottie.

"This was our sophomore year. We helped design the theme, and your mom made our skirts. One of the student's parents loaned the 1955 Convertible Red Thunderbird for us to use as a photo prop." Miranda explained.

"Well, that explains why it is in a building," Abigail said. "Did Scottie and I date?"

"No," Miranda answered. "He was the quarterback for the varsity football team, and dated Amy, the captain of the cheer squad."

"I can see that." Abigail said.

"What do you mean?" Miranda asked.

"Look at him. He is cute, and most football players date the cheerleaders, right? I don't know much but I know that I am not the uptight, high maintenance, it's all about me type of person." Abigail stated.

"Are you sure you don't remember because you just sounded just like the Abigail that I know." Miranda inquired.

They were both laughing when Mr. Arnold walked in. "Now that is the sound I miss. You two girls are laughing and having a good time together. How are your parents?" He asked as he placed his items on the desk in the entryway.

"Everyone is doing well," Miranda answered.

"Please send them my grateful gratitude for everything they did for us after the accident. I have thanked them multiple times, but I could never thank you all enough," he said.

"Yes sir, I will let them know," she said.

"Well, I am going to let you girls get back to it. I am going to eat and then off to the shower," he said as he walked to the kitchen.

"Yes sir," Abigail said.

"If I don't see you before you leave, it's good to have you over. Don't be a stranger," he said.

"Thank you. Good to see you too," Miranda said. "Just like old times." She shook her head. "Now where were we?"

"Why was I in the picture and not Amy?" Abigail asked.

"They had a game that Friday night, and she tore her ACL in one of the cheer techniques, so she couldn't attend the dance. Which did not hurt my feelings at all," Miranda answered.

"I am sensing you didn't like her much." Abigail said.

"That is an understatement. I could not stand her. She is whiny, complains about everything, spoiled, and must be the center of attention. I wanted to knock her out almost every time we got together. I am shocked they stayed together as long as they did." Miranda explained.

"Why?" Abigail asked.

"He is very protective of you, and it didn't matter who it was, they knew not to mess with you. But Amy pushed her limits too many times. It just blew my mind that he didn't send her packing." Miranda answered.

"Sounds like he loves her a lot, and just overlooked her flaws." Abigail inquired.

"You don't even remember her, and yet you are still defending her." Miranda replied. Abigail gave her a puzzled look. "I'm sorry. It's just that you have always defended her when I could have just knocked her lights out. That is why I think this night was one of my favorites because she wasn't there to ruin everyone's mood." Miranda added.

"I think you may be over-exaggerating about her a little bit." Abigail said.

"I am serious. It was that bad, and if you were not around to help me control myself, there is no telling what would have happened." Miranda stated.

"So how did the night go without her there?" Abigail pressed on.

"I've never seen Scottie so relaxed and engaged with everyone before. He didn't have to worry about anyone being petty about everything. Whether it was a friend or someone worse, he could give you the slightest attention without any hassle." Miranda said. "We all tried to talk him into breaking up with her that night, but he just kept denying his feelings. Even though we could all see how you would look at one another, and act around each other. You two were just stubborn and denied it every time someone mentioned it. Even on this very night, we saw it, but he just denied it once more. I believe this was one of the best nights for him though."

"I wish I could remember." Abigail said.

"If you want, we can hang out together. I am certain that between your therapy sessions, and my reminiscing about our times together. We could make it happen," Miranda assured.

Abigail perked up. "You don't mind? Do you think it would help?"

"I believe it is worth a shot. What can it hurt? Plus, I would be spending time with my best friend again." Miranda said. Abigail leaped and hugged her.

Miranda and Abigail spent as much time as they could together going over the photos and telling her stories. They had been doing their sessions as much as possible over the last few weeks. The therapists said that it was great they were rekindling their friendship, and that it was helping Abigail on her path to recovery.

"Abigail, your mom and I were wondering if you would like to have a summer splash here at the house?" Mr. Arnold asked as he poured himself a cup of coffee.

"I would like that," Abigail exclaimed. "It's perfect timing since Miranda will be starting college soon."

"That is great news. We were thinking of inviting the Harmon's and Johnson's as well. Would that be okay?" He asked.

"Sure, maybe being around them will help knock something in my brain around to connect all the loose marbles." She stated.

"Great! I will let your mom know, and we can start planning. Maybe we can have it this weekend since we are both off." He stated.

"I will call Miranda, and she can invite others too. If that is okay." She added.

"Sure, it will be great to have others around. Just make sure she lets them know not to overwhelm you." He said.

"I am good, Dad. I trust her." She assured.

"Great to hear your friendship is being restored." He said.

"She is an amazing person." She added.

"You two are peas in a pod." He stated.

"Oh, Dad," she giggled.

"I am going to head to work. I will discuss this with your mom on my way. We can all touch base one night this week," he told her as he placed his shield on his belt.

"Yes sir." She replied.

He leaned down and hugged her. "I love you. Have a great day."

"I love you too. Be safe," she called out as he headed for the door.

Abigail called Miranda, excited to tell her the news. Miranda couldn't get her hello out before Abigail interrupted, "Guess what?"

"What?" Miranda asked.

"We are going to have a summer splash. Just like the one you were telling me about the other day." She said excitedly.

"Yay!" Miranda screamed.

"I would like you to invite all of our friends." She continued.

"Are you sure?" Miranda asked.

"Yes! I think it will be fun getting reacquainted with them again." Abigail replied.

"I can do that if you are sure you are up for it." Miranda agreed.

"Most definitely." Abigail added.

"Do you have the date and time?"

"Not yet, but I should know by tomorrow night."

"Just text me when you have the information, and I will take care of the rest."

"Wonderful. I am so excited!" Abigail exclaimed.

"I can tell."

"I will talk to you later. I must get dressed for my physical therapy appointment."

"How much longer do you have?" Miranda inquired.

"I believe two more weeks. I am getting my strength and mobility back, but I am still scared to overwork it."

"That is understandable. You will be good as new once they are completed."

"I hope so."

"I am going to let you go, so you won't be late."

"Okay, bye." Abigail dismissed.

"Bye."

Abigail ended the call and squealed with excitement. "This is going to be so much fun!"

*Count on Me – Bruno Mars*

# CHAPTER 16

## I Remembered

The summer splash was planned, and everyone was invited. Friday night was upon them, and Miranda was staying over to assist in getting everything ready. Abigail still didn't have full mobility in her left arm, and it was hard for her to do any heavy lifting.

"We have all the food and drinks purchased. Everything is ready," Mrs. Mia said as she finished prepping all the food for the splash.

"I have cleaned the pool and hot tub, stacked the firewood for the firepit, and finished all the lawn maintenance," Mr. Arnold called out as he headed upstairs for a shower.

"How about you girls?" Mrs. Mia asked as Miranda and Abigail walked in through the back door.

"We cleaned and stocked the game room, and we are grabbing fresh sheets for the bed," Abigail answered as she entered the laundry room.

"I believe the others will be here by noon to help get everything set up," Mrs. Mia said. The girls were walking through the kitchen to the back door. "I will let you guys sleep in tomorrow, so just check in when you are up," Mrs. Mia answered. Abigail opened the back door for Miranda. "We are here if y'all need anything."

"Yes, ma'am," Abigail said.

"Have fun," she called out as Abigail was about to close the door.

They were walking the lit stone pathway to the game room. "This feels like old times," Miranda said.

"Maybe soon I will be able to agree with you," Abigail said. She opened the door to the game room. It smelt clean and fresh.

"I agree. I know that the therapy and our get-togethers are working." Miranda agreed.

"With everyone being here, it may help my memory return." Abigail stated.

"It has been so long since we all have been together. I am so excited!" Miranda said joyfully.

"I hope others will understand my condition. I am more worried about Scottie coming."

"Why?" Miranda inquired.

"This will be the first time we have been together since the accident. What if he and I don't reconcile like you and I?" Abigail explained.

"You and him with the what-ifs! Just let things fall as they are supposed to."

"What do you mean by our what-ifs?"

"That is all I heard from him while you were in a coma. What if this what if that, and now you are starting with the what-ifs. It is so overwhelming listening to y'all worry over things you cannot control. I am not sure how you cope with all those." Miranda explained.

"Maybe Amy will keep his attention off me so that he won't notice my weirdness."

"Amy?"

"Yes. Don't you think he will bring his girlfriend?" Abigail added.

"Oh my. With all the stories and everything I forgot to tell you."

"Tell me what?"

They sat down on the loveseat. "As I have told you before, Scottie is very protective of you, and Amy likes to push her limits." She explained.

"I remember you telling me that." Abigail said.

"After your accident, she picked fights with him about how much time he was spending at the hospital. He had enough of it and called it off with her. I couldn't have been happier myself."

"I understand why you would, but how did Scottie feel about it?"

"He told me he was relieved to finally have his life back and could concentrate on his wants."

"I just hope that I don't act weird around everyone." Abigail said with concern.

"Just be yourself like you have with me. If you start feeling anxious or overwhelmed, I will take care of it." Miranda assured.

"Thank you so much for being here and having patience with me."

"You are lucky. I only have patience with you because you are my best friend," Miranda confessed. The girls both laughed.

"How about a movie or a game?"

"A movie sounds good."

"A Walk to Remember? I haven't watched this before, if I have, I don't remember."

"We have watched it together. It is one of our favorites."

"We don't have to watch it again if you don't want to." Abigail stated.

"No, it's okay. We can watch it. Just let me get some comfortable clothes on." Miranda grabbed her bag of clothes and went to the bathroom.

"That sounds like a good idea. I will change also, but I am going to fix us a snack." She opened the freezer. "Would you like some pizza rolls or just a bowl of popcorn?"

"Pizza rolls…" Miranda said.

"I know with ranch dressing," Abigail interrupted her before she could finish her sentence. Miranda swung open the bathroom door. Abigail turned around with her eyes and mouth wide open, "I remembered!" Abigail screamed. The girls started screaming and jumping up and down.

"You remembered!" Miranda squealed. Miranda pressed the intercom to call to the house, "Mr. Arnold, Mrs. Mia, come quick!" she squealed over the intercom. They were still jumping up and down when they came bursting through the door.

"What is it?" Mr. Arnold asked as they came closer to them.

"Abigail, are you okay?" Mrs. Mia asked.

"Yes ma'am," she said with tears streaming down their faces.

"Well don't leave us in suspense. Tell us what is going on," Mr. Arnold insisted.

"I remembered something. It isn't much," Abigail said, wiping her tears with her shirt.

They screamed and joined the girls. Mr. Arnold wrapped his arms around them and squeezed them into a group hug. "It doesn't matter how small it is. This is worth rejoicing," he stated.

"Dear, you are smothering us," Mrs. Mia said to her husband.

"Oh, I am sorry. I don't know my own strength," he said, letting them go.

"Tell us what you remembered," Mrs. Mia said.

"I remembered that Miranda likes ranch dressing with her pizza rolls," she answered.

"How did it happen?" Mr. Arnold asked, clearing the tears from the lens of his glasses with the bottom of his t-shirt.

"I was getting our snacks together to watch a movie, and I asked her what she wanted," Abigail explained.

"I answered pizza rolls." Miranda cut in.

"I said I know, with ranch dressing," Abigail said with a crack in her voice, and tears streaming down her face.

"All of the hard work is paying off," Mr. Arnold said.

"This is so exciting!" Mrs. Mia squealed with tears flowing down her face. "I am going to call the therapist to share the good news. She told us this is how your memory could return. A little at a time, or it may come to you all at once like a rush of memories."

"Keep it up, girls," Mr. Arnold smiled as he held the door for Mrs. Mia. "She is so excited that she forgot to tell y'all good night. Rest well, girls," he giggled as he closed the door behind him.

"I can't believe it. I feel like I am dreaming," Abigail said.

"I know, my heart is pounding," Miranda agreed, with her hand over her heart. "Maybe the movie will help us calm down," she said. She leaned over and placed the movie on the Xbox.

"I don't know if I can calm down." Abigail said.

"We don't have to watch it if you want to do something else." Miranda added.

"No, I want to watch it. Maybe it can help me remember something else, but I would like to change into my comfortable clothes. Do you mind microwaving the pizza rolls, since we got distracted?" Abigail asked as she grabbed her bag and went into the bathroom.

"I like the way you think. I will take care of the pizza rolls." Miranda stated.

They finished the movie. Both were crying at the end of the movie. "I need to go to bed. All this crying has made me tired," Abigail said.

"I agree," Miranda said. They pulled the cushions off the loveseat and pulled out the hideaway bed.

"I hope I can have someone love me like Landon loves Jamie," Abigail said, as she threw a corner of the sheets to Miranda's side. Miranda dropped the sheet.

"Are you pulling my leg or something?" Miranda asked.

"No. Why are you looking at me that way?" Abigail inquired.

"Because you said the same thing the last time we watched it." Miranda stated.

"Really?" Abigail asked, puzzled.

"Yes, and I told you that you do have someone that loves you like that, but you would not accept it." Miranda explained.

"Oh wow, who is this mysterious person?" Abigail inquired. She fluffed her pillow and climbed under the sheets.

"Scottie Harmon."

"What? No way. I thought we were all best friends."

Miranda cut off the lights and climbed into bed. "We are, but you two have always danced around your feelings for one another. Everyone else already knew what you two wouldn't admit."

"How do you know his feelings for me have not changed?" Abigail asked, curiously.

"Because I know Scottie, and he has been crazy about you since the ninth grade. He calls to check up on our progress daily. He doesn't want to interfere with your recovery and is willing to wait to see you on your own terms. He is playing all tough, but I can hear it in his voice," Miranda explained. She lay down on her pillow.

"I didn't mean to hurt anyone. I wish I still had my memory. It was very lonely before we started our process. Yes, I talked to my friends in San Antonio, but having someone in person is different." Abigail explained.

"The accident wasn't your fault. No one blames you for anything," Miranda said. She fell silent. Tears began to fill her eyes, and slowly streamed down her face. "It has been lonely for me as well. Of course, I have had a boyfriend to talk to, but you are my best friend. When we almost lost you..." her voice cracked, and she swallowed to clear it. "That was the scariest moment of my life. When you woke from the coma was the happiest moment for me. I know you didn't remember me, but deep down, I knew our friendship would see us through anything," she wiped her tears.

"And look at us now soaking our pillows with our tears together," Abigail said. She reached and grabbed Miranda's hand. They squeezed tight.

"Let's get some rest and stop worrying about tomorrow. We all understand the situation, and we all love you regardless. No one blames you for anything." Miranda said.

"Thank you for comforting me and listening to me. I am grateful to have you as my best friend."

Miranda tapped her hand, and then let it go. "That is what best friends are for. Now get some sleep, it's been a long day."

The room fell silent, but Abigail couldn't fall asleep. Her mind was racing about all the things that may go wrong tomorrow. *Was I always like this, worrying over things I have no control over?* She thought to herself. *Maybe this is another effect of the accident.* She tossed and turned for a few more hours trying to clear her mind. She finally drifted off to sleep.

# CHAPTER 17

## The Introduction

Her alarm started going off at ten o'clock in the morning. She stretched and got out of bed. *I don't know if I should wake her up or let her sleep. How do I wake her up? Is she one of those that throws punches if she is startled in her sleep? If only I could remember. Oh well, here goes nothing.*

"Miranda, it's time to get up," she spoke softly.

"What time is it," Miranda asked as she stretched.

"Ten o'clock." She replied.

"Oh my, this is the latest I have slept in a long time," Miranda said, as she set up in bed.

"Are you okay if I go get dressed?" She asked.

"I can grab a bite to eat and wake up while I wait." Miranda answered.

"I won't be long."

Miranda put up the pullout bed and placed the pillows on the couch with the folded comforter. She was almost finished eating a bowl of fruity pebbles when Abigail came out of the bathroom.

"It's all yours."

She took her last two bites and threw the paper bowl and plastic spoon away. “I will be out in a jiffy,” she said, grabbing her bag.

“Take your time,” Abigail said. She opened the pantry trying to decide what to have for breakfast- a bowl of cereal, or a muffin with orange juice. *I think I will go with the banana nut muffin and orange juice.* She sat down at the bar to eat. She was halfway through her muffin when Miranda came out. She was lost in her thoughts and was pinching off small bites of the muffin.

“You are moving slowly like a sloth. Are you okay?”

“Oh yeah. I was just thinking.” Abigail replied.

“You aren’t overthinking, are you? If you aren’t ready for everyone to come, I can call them and cancel.”

“No, please don’t. I am excited, but just a little nervous.”

“It will be fine. I will be right by your side.”

“Girls, are y’all awake?” Mrs. Mia asked over the intercom.

“Good morning,” Abigail answered.

“It is almost eleven o’clock and the others will be here in the next forty-five minutes or so. I just wanted to make sure y’all were up and moving around. Do y’all mind assisting me with getting the outside bar set up?” Mrs. Mia asked.

“Sure. We will be right out.” Abigail replied.

Everyone got to work. The girls set up the tables. Mrs. Mia organized the bar. Mr. Arnold fired up the charcoal in the grill. Once they were finished with their duties they went and lay by the pool.

Scottie was taking his time to get dressed. Stacey was rushing him. She was excited to be going back to the Whittinger’s.

He was as well, but she didn't remember him. It hurts just thinking about it. *How am I supposed to act when she doesn't even know who I am? I wish I could just run to her and tell her how I feel. I can't do that; it would probably drive her away even farther than she already is. Don't you remember how well it worked out for Leo in "The Vow"? I would wait for Abigail just like he did for Paige. I kind of already have. I just have to have patience.* He had his Hawaiian swim trunks on and was trying to find the right shirt to wear. He opened his drawer and found his baby blue American Eagle t-shirt. *Perfect.* He ran his hands through his curls. *No need to put any product in it. I will be sweating and swimming.* He looked at his reflection in the mirror.

"Everything is going to be fine," Mrs. Trudy said. She startled him, and he spun and saw her standing in the doorway.

"I just don't know how to act around her. I haven't seen or talked to her in so long." He stated.

"Just be the great guy you are, and everything will be fine." She assured

"Come on! You can't do anything to help your looks, so stop staring in the mirror," Stacy teased as she fell across his bed.

"Calm down. We have plenty of time. We practically live next door. It will only take us a matter of seconds to get there."

"I am ready to go now. I can smell the grill cooking when I step outside, it's calling to us to hurry up." She sat up on the side of the bed and gestured toward the window.

"I guess there is no use in prolonging this any longer. Let's go," Scottie said.

"Dad, lover boy is finally ready, so we can leave now!" Stacy screamed as she pushed off the bed and made her way to the door.

"Cut it out, Stacy. I will hear no more of this," Mrs. Trudy said.

"I was only teasing." She stated.

"I mean it, no more." Mrs. Trudy gave her a stern look.

"Yes ma'am." Stacy waited at the front door for everyone.

The Johnson's arrived before the Harmon's. The girls were still out by the pool. Scottie became more nervous the closer they got to the Whittingers'. Once they reached the backyard he walked over to the grill where the men were standing. He glanced over to the pool and saw Abigail and Miranda lying in the lounge chairs. His heart started to beat faster. He was worried they could see it through his thin shirt. He felt as if he couldn't take another step; like his legs had completely stopped working.

"Scottie! Wait for me," Stacy called out behind him.

Abigail looked up when she heard Stacy scream Scottie's name. She leaned over to Miranda, "I told you he would bring his new girlfriend," she whispered. Miranda looked over to where Scottie and Stacy were standing by the grill. Miranda busted out in a burst of laughter.

"What is so funny?" Abigail asked.

"Abigail, that is his little sister, Stacy." Miranda corrected.

"Oh wow, I feel foolish." She said.

"You didn't know, so don't start attacking yourself. Don't worry you will meet everyone today." Miranda assured.

Abigail looked back at them. "Oh, I can see the resemblance now." She and Scottie made eye contact, and she turned away from his glance. Her stomach was filling up with butterflies. She leaned over to Miranda once more and whispered, "I am going to have issues with him."

"How do you know that? You haven't even spoken to him yet?" Miranda asked.

"He is even better looking in person. Those pictures didn't do him any justice. If he keeps looking at me like that, I won't be able to control myself." She explained.

"Oh, my word. I am starting to wish the old Abigail was back." Miranda stated.

"Why would you say a thing like that?" Abigail asked, nudging Miranda on the arm.

"Because you kept all those thoughts to yourself. I prefer not to hear the mushy crush you have on him. I don't see him the same as you," Miranda said. She shook like she was trying to get something disgusting off her. "Disgusting."

"Stop it," Abigail said. She and Miranda started to laugh once more.

Scottie heard her laughter; it was something he missed so much. "It feels good to see her laughing and doing well," he said.

"Yes. She and Miranda have been going through the binder of photos and she has been telling her stories to help her regain her memory," Mr. Arnold said. He flipped the burgers over. "And last night, we had a small breakthrough."

"Really? What happened?" Mr. Johnson asked.

"The girls were in the game getting ready to watch a movie. Abigail asked Miranda what she wanted. When Miranda said pizza rolls, Abigail said with ranch dressing. It was completely out of memory. They called us screaming over the intercom. Scared us to death." He chuckled, placing his hand over his heart. "Until we ran and found out the great news. We believe the time with Miranda is helping her regain her memory. Thank y'all for letting her come around, and do the sessions," he said to Mr. Johnson.

"We are glad that their time together has rekindled their friendship. Miranda has her spark back. It took a toll on her not being able to see or talk to her. We are truly excited that she is doing so well," Mr. Johnson assured.

"I can relate," Scottie said. His dad gave him a pat on the back.

"He mopes around like a child who lost his puppy," Stacy teased.

Scottie's cheeks turned red with heat.

"Stacy, remember what your mom said before we left?" Mr. Matthew spoke sternly.

"Yes, sir." Stacy said.

"I expect you to obey her orders." Mr. Matthew added.

"Yes sir." She replied.

"We are happy to hear the great news," Mr. Matthew continued.

"But she doesn't remember us?" Scottie asked.

"No, I am sorry. She is excited that y'all were coming today," Mr. Arnold answered. "I can walk you over and introduce you if you would like."

"Yes, please I have missed seeing her," Stacy said.

"Right this way," Mr. Arnold said, pointing them in the direction of the pool.

Scottie's heart was breaking. *I am going to be introduced to her like a stranger.* Mr. Arnold cut through his thoughts.

"We ask that there is no horse playing. We don't want to have a setback for her or for her to injure her arm," he explained quietly.

Scottie and Stacy nodded in agreement. “We understand, sir,” Scottie said. He forced the smile on his face as they came upon the girls.

“Abigail, this is Scottie and Stacy Harmon. They live down the street from us,” Mr. Arnold stated. *Neighbor? I can’t believe I have gone from her best friend to just a neighbor.* He reached out his hand and smiled as he shook her hand.

“Hello. Nice to meet you,” he said with the best smile he could force. Hoping his hand was sweating like he was.

“Hi, Abigail,” Stacy said.

Abigail’s butterflies were now spinning and making her nauseous. “Hello,” she said with a smile.

“Okay, well I am heading back to the grill. The burgers should be ready in about twenty minutes,” Mr. Arnold said. “You guys enjoy yourselves.”

“Thanks, Dad,” Abigail said.

“So, are we able to swim or do we have to wait till after we eat?” Stacy asked. Scottie nudged her with his elbow. “What? I am just wondering if I can swim,” Stacy explained.

“It’s okay, Scottie. Of course, you can swim. We were just sun tanning while waiting for everyone to arrive,” Miranda answered.

Scottie and Abigail locked eyes once more, and she smiled. He smiled back. “Maybe getting in the pool isn’t a bad idea. We have been lying here for a good hour or so,” Abigail said.

“What are we waiting for? Let’s go!” Stacy said.

Abigail stood in the shallow part of the water to cool off. She feared that if she started to swim it would overwork her arm, and she wouldn’t be able to enjoy the company. Now that she saw

Scottie in person, she wanted to get to know him. *Those pictures didn't do him any justice,* she thought to herself. Scottie went and stood next to her.

"Your dad was telling us that you remembered that Miranda liked ranch with her pizza rolls last night." He stated.

"Yeah. It's not that big, but it does get my hopes up that maybe all these sessions are paying off." Abigail stated.

"He also told us that Miranda is telling you stories to help you recollect your memories." Scottie said.

"She did tell me last night about Amy. I am sorry about the breakup." Abigail said.

Scottie shook his head and turned to face the opposite direction. He ran his fingers through his curls, before resting his arms on the side of the pool. "She could have left her out of the stories. You don't have to apologize. My life has been very peaceful."

"Wow, she must have been a character with the way you and Miranda talk about her." She stated.

"You have no idea, but that is over now." He agreed.

"Hey, guys," Avey called out as he approached them. "Mind if I join?"

"Of course," Miranda smiled as she swam to meet him at the stairs of the pool. "Abigail, this is my boyfriend, Avey."

"Nice to meet you," Abigail said, and held out her hand to shake his.

"Likewise," he said with a smile. "Hey, bud" He shook Scottie's hand and pulled him in for a bro friend hug.

"Hello." He returned to Abigail's side.

"Who else is coming?" Avey asked.

"This is it," Miranda answered.

"What happened to everyone else?" Abigail asked. The guys turned in shock at one another. Thinking she had just remembered something. "What?"

"Guys she has been looking at our photos and there are several group pictures. She thought the entire group would be here. Well minus one of course," Miranda smirked at Scottie.

"Ha, ha," he sneered.

"I invited everyone, but Xavier had to work…." Miranda stated.

"Ricky and Mari-Kate are on a cruise with Amy and her new boyfriend," Scottie interrupted.

"Are you keeping tabs, bro," Avey joked. He and Miranda joined them in the shallow end of the pool.

"No, that was planned before graduation. I would have been there but…" Scottie explained.

"If not for me," Abigail interrupted.

Avey looked confused. "Did I miss something? How are you to blame?" He asked.

"She's not. What I was going to say was, I came to my senses," he said with a smile. "It is not your fault."

"Exactly!" Miranda said. "I have told her that, but maybe it will set in since it is coming from you."

"It's alright because we are here and we are going to have a blast," Avey said.

"I agree," Miranda said.

“Alright, everyone. Time to eat,” Mr. Arnold shouted.

# CHAPTER 18

## Asking for Permission

Everyone gathered around the bar fixing their plates. The adults sat on one end of the table, and the others joined Abigail and Miranda at the other end. Everyone ate and enjoyed the fellowship with one another. Once everyone was done eating, they decided to play a few games of Just Dance on the Xbox to let their food settle.

They were divided into two groups, boys against girls. The boys felt confident and weren't worried that they would be outnumbered. They were having so much fun and it felt like old times when they had gotten together at the Whittinger's. Abigail was just being herself. Though she acted a little differently, it wasn't in a bad way. Scottie liked the new Abby. She wasn't scared to speak her mind and flirted back with him. He enjoyed seeing her laugh again.

It was a tie. They chose Abigail and Scottie to go head to head for the tiebreaker. Scottie let Abigail choose the song, and she chose "One Thing by One Direction" for the battle song. They were doing great, and she was keeping up with him with every move. Three minutes into the game, her arm had become tired. It was starting to burn, so she missed a few of the hand jesters. She couldn't keep up with her avatar. The hours of playing were taking a toll, but she wasn't letting him or anyone else know. It cost her points and Scottie won the game. Though he knew that she had slowed down in the end. She teased him for cheating, and he dealt it right back.

"Can we please go swimming now?" Stacy pleaded.

"Sounds good to me. I need to cool off after all this dancing," Abigail said. She wanted to get her arm in the cool water to ease the pain. "Man, I don't need physical therapy. I can just come out here for an hour or so and work my arm with this game." She joked.

"Are you feeling okay?" Scottie asked.

"I am fine. Thank you for asking." She smiled at him.

His heart skipped a beat. Abigail stepped down into the water. It was nice and cool. It felt so good on her arm. She went in about four feet deep this time to where it wasn't too deep, and leaned against the side of the pool. Scottie swam to the deep and back of the pool to cool off.

"I know I didn't win that battle fair and square." He stated.

"Really? What makes you think I would let you win?" she asked.

"I know you would never let anyone win. You are too competitive for that. That's how I know you pushed yourself to the point of overworking your arm. I could see you easing up at the end of the song." He explained.

"So, are you suggesting we go at it again?" She inquired.

"Yes, but not with anything that you have to use your left arm in." He answered.

"What exactly do you have in mind?" She asked.

"I brought our bocce game, and I think it is perfect for a tiebreaker. Do you remember how to play?" He asked.

"Yes, we played in P.E. when I was in San Antonio," she answered. "You are aware that Miranda and I were on the softball team, correct? Or were you hoping I didn't know that," she teased him. Throwing him a flirtatious smile.

"I am aware. Just as I am sure you are aware Avey and I play football," he teased back. "That should be a fair game then, correct?"

"This is true," she agreed. She waved her arms under the water to make small circular currents in the water. She was trying to distract herself from his glare. She was scared that it was getting harder and harder to resist her emotions when she looked into his eyes. “So when should we do this rematch?” She asked, without looking up from the water.

“Let your arm rest, and we can do it a little later. We haven’t been in the water long enough for you to relax.” He answered.

“What if I said I am ready now?” She turned to look at him. She forgot they were standing close, and their skin touched. Electricity flew through her body, and she shivered.

“You just say the word, and we can grab the others,” he said without moving away from her touch. *He doesn’t seem to mind being this close to me,* she thought. She turned to see that Avey and Miranda were sitting at the deep end with their feet in the water.

“Hey, Scottie wants a rematch. He thinks that it wasn’t a fair match before. He suggested a game of Bocce. What do y’all think? Should we give them another chance?”

“Stop going soft on me, man. We won that battle fair and square,” Avey joked.

“Do I have to? I would like to swim,” Stacy said.

“I think that will be fine, Stacy,” Abigail said. Stacy went back to swimming and enjoyed the entire pool to herself.

“Well, that would make it even, and fair,” Miranda said.

“We have nothing to fear,” Scottie answered.

“Oh, I see that you forgot all about the tossing match between the boys and girls at the county fair that year,” Miranda chuckled.

“Tossing match? I don’t remember that story, but it sounds interesting. Who won?” Abigail chuckled.

“We didn’t get to that story, but we can later. The girls of course,” Miranda affirmed.

“That game was rigged, and y’all know it,” Scottie said.

"You keep telling yourself that, but the girls won that night. We are going to win tonight," Miranda taunted.

"Maybe you should be there when she tells the story. You know, so you can defend your side of the story," Abigail teased.

Scottie smiled. "I just might take you up on that offer. I do have a reputation to protect."

"What reputation? We aren't in high school anymore?" Miranda ragged.

"Hey, she still doesn't remember, so I still have to impress her," Scottie said, defending himself.

"Seems to be doing good so far," Abigail realized she spoke the words out loud. Her cheeks flushed with embarrassment.

"See, I am still on top of my game," he teased. Smiling at her.

"What game?" Avey laughed. Scottie turned and they started passing boxing jabs between the two of them.

"Okay. Cool the male testosterone. Are we going to play before it is too dark?" Miranda asked.

"Yes, let me go grab it." He ran off to grab the game, and the others walked to the grass area to wait for him to return. Miranda nudged Abigail.

"What?" Abigail asked.

"I saw you flirting with him." Miranda stated.

"If he wants to dish it out, so can I," Abigail said. "I didn't realize he was so much fun to be around. He has the entire package."

"Entire package?" Miranda asked, puzzled.

"Yeah, you know the looks, personality, confidence, humor, and is kind," Abigail said. "I just hope he feels the same way.

"From the looks of it he isn't holding back," Miranda said.

"Sorry," Scottie said. Abigail jumped not realizing that he was coming up behind them. "I will toss the pallino ball to start the game. We will play teams, so girls select your color." He placed the set on the ground in front of them. Miranda and Abigail were discussing the two colors. They bent down and collected the red balls. "Okay, Avey and I are green."

Scottie and Avey collected their balls after Scottie tossed the pallino a good distance from them. He started going over the rules of the game with them. "The team with the highest points wins. The points won't be collected until both teams have thrown their last ball," Scottie said. He drew a line in the grass with the heel of his foot in front of them. He then walked past the pallino ball a little way and created another line with his foot. "The line here is the out-of-bounds line." He started walking back toward them. "The line here in front is the line to toss from. All tosses must be underhand. We are supposed to toss a coin to see who starts, but if Avey is okay with it I say let the girls go first."

"It's cool with me," Avey said.

"We have this," Abigail said. She waited for Scottie to move behind her so she would not hit him. She drew back her right hand and tossed her first ball. It rolled to the left of the pallino and stopped. "I believe that is a good first toss, correct? I have lost my memory so I may be wrong," she teased, as she turned and looked at him while moving from the line.

"Not bad, not bad at all," he said. He stepped up to the line and tossed his ball. You heard the loud crack as it hit Abigail's ball and pushed it a little further from the pallino. "Yes," he shouted, yanking his right arm toward him with a fist pump.

"Don't get so excited. We are just getting started," Miranda said. She gave him a slight, playful shove to move him from the toss line. She tossed her ball, and it rolled to the right, next to the pallino. "How is that?" She teased.

"Alright, Alright, enough of that," Avey said as he made his way to toss his ball. "How about a good luck kiss," he teased Miranda, puckering up his lips at her.

"No way! You're the enemy. I am not helping you," she chuckled, pushing his face away from her.

He looked over to Scottie. "Don't look at me, bro. I am surely not kissing you." They all laughed.

Avey tossed the ball and it smacked Scottie's ball so hard that it rolled out of bounds.

"DEAD BALL!" Abigail cheered.

"What?" Avey asked.

"Yeah, you hit my ball out of bounds, so it doesn't count anymore. Therefore, it is called a dead ball," Scottie said. "You do know that we are on teams, and the point is to hit their red balls, not your teammates, right," Scottie joked. "You are making us look bad," he giggled.

"You throw the balls, I catch them. I am out of my league here," Avey said as he walked to stand by Miranda.

"It's alright. We still have one more chance. We can still win this," Scottie said. "Alright, Abby. Show us what you've got," he teased as he stepped out of her way.

"Abby?" Abigail looked at him as she passed by.

"Sorry, it's a habit. I won't call you that if it bothers you," Scottie apologized.

"No, I like it," she said with a smile. He let out a sigh of relief. Abigail gave her ball a toss. It rolled in front of the pallino and stopped. "Ha, let's see if you can do better than that." Abigail teased.

"I know I can. Step aside and let me show you how it's done," Scottie said. He tossed his ball and there was crack, crack. His ball hit Abigail's ball and made it now touch the pallino. "Oh, no!" he screamed, clasping his fingers together on the top of his head.

Abigail leaned over to him. "I believe that is known as a kiss," she said, making eye contact with Scottie. His heart started beating hard. She could probably hear it as she stood so close to him. *Oh my, she is flirting with me. I have never seen her act this way, but I like it,* he thought to himself. "Well, that is if I remember correctly," she said with a slight smirk.

"Yes, it is called a kiss," he said, giving her a big smile.

Avey gestured toward Abigail with his thumb, "Is it me or is she flirting with him," he whispered to Miranda.

"Oh, she is flirting alright," Miranda said. "Okay, move along," she called out to Scottie, waving her hand as if to say 'move'. Her tossed ball rolled to the left of the pallino and stopped close to Scottie's ball.

"So close but no cigar," Avey said as they passed, and he blew her a kiss. Miranda rolled her eyes and shook her head.

"We will see about that," Abigail said.

Avey tossed his ball and it smacked into her first ball, knocking it out of bounds. "Dead ball," he called out.

"Okay, let's count the points," Scottie said.

They walked over to view the balls. Abigail counted. "We won!" she squealed.

"Wait, how can you say that?" Avey asked.

"Miranda has a ball on each side of the pallino. That is two points. I have the "kissing" ball, which is two more points." She paused and winked at Scottie. "Giving us a total of four points. We won!" Miranda leaned over and hugged her neck.

"I tried to warn y'all, but guys and their egos," Miranda teased.

"It's okay," Scottie said as he patted Avey on the back. "It isn't the first, and I am certain it won't be the last."

"We get it! You can stop rubbing it in our faces," Avey said. Referring to the girls doing a celebration dance like they made a touchdown.

"Sorry, not sorry," Miranda teased. They all started picking up the game and putting it back in its bag. Once it was all picked up, they began walking back toward the pool area.

"Scottie, we are heading home. Do you wanna come now or will you be home later?" Mr. Matthew asked.

Scottie looked over at Abigail, "are you okay with me staying longer?"

"Of course," she said with a smile.

"Can you give me a ride home when you leave?" Scottie asked Avey.

"Sure," Avey said.

"Avey is going to bring me home later," Scottie answered.

It was getting dark, and the solar lights were coming on, lighting the stone paths. The pool was also lit up with the lights under the water. The Johnson's and Harmon's left at the same time, leaving only Avey, Miranda, and Scottie at the Whittinger's.

"Would y'all like to chill in the pool for a little while?" Abigail asked.

"I believe that is a great idea," Miranda said. "Beat ya," she nudged Avey. They took off running and did cannon balls in the pool. Waves went so high and splashed around the pool.

"What are they? Ten years old?" Scottie asked.

"It's okay, let them have fun," Abigail said.

"It's better to be safe than sorry. What if you slip in the water?" He asked.

"I will be okay, I promise. You want to get two mats and float in the shallow end?" She asked.

"Sounds good," he answered.

She ran to the shed and grabbed two of the foam mats for them. She stopped by the drinks and grabbed them each a drink.

"Oh, thank you," he said as she handed him the drink and his mat.

They placed their drink on the side of the pool, so they could get on their mats. Scottie held her mat to assist her get on the mat. Once she was on her mat, he handed her their drinks to hold until he was on his mat. After several tries, he finally was able to get on the mat without flipping it.

"Harder than it looks," he laughed. Shaking his head like a dog straight out of a bath. Abigail squealed as he splashed her with the cold water. "My bad," he winked.

"Would you like your drink now?" She asked.

"Sure, if you promise not to flip me. You look like you are planning something devious." He teased.

"I promise, because if you go over, I may go over as well." She said.

He paddled his mat over to where she was. He grabbed her mat and pulled her over by his, and she handed him his drink. They both popped open their cans. "Let's hold onto each other's mats so we don't drift apart." He said.

"So smart," she teased him. She grabbed his mat with her left hand, and he held onto hers with his left hand. "I didn't believe it when Miranda told me you were protective over me, but I think I got a glimpse of it back there."

"I wish I could have protected you the night of the accident," he said softly.

"Hey, if I am not allowed to blame myself, then neither are you. Agree?" She said.

"That is hard to do." He added.

"I agree, but everyone is right. We can't keep living in the past. Holding onto guilt. Today has shown me that I am blessed with great people in my life, and I should stop moping and being by myself. I mean, when I started hanging out with Miranda it brought light back into my life. Before that, I didn't know how to cope with living in a place I didn't remember. I didn't even remember moving away from my friends in San Antonio. I would cry myself to sleep many nights, but my joy started returning and I could laugh again. Now, I want to get out of bed, instead of laying in it all day. I don't want to lose that again." She explained.

"Abby, I am sorry for not being there for you, but I didn't want to interfere with your recovery. You never lost any of us. We were just waiting patiently for you to be ready for us in your life once more. I promise that you will never lose me," he said. He placed his hand over hers, and she opened her hand to hold his. They lay there in silence enjoying the moment with one another.

"This feels so right," Abigail whispered.

"Yes, it does." Scottie agreed.

Miranda and Avey stopped horse-playing in the deep end when they saw them holding hands. "What is going on over there?" Avey whispered.

"You know as much as I know." Miranda answered.

"She is different, but not in a bad way. I like the new Abigail." Avey stated.

"I do too, but it's hard to adjust when my friend isn't the same as she used to be." She said.

"I know, but we must accept that she may never recover her memory. Although, I believe this could be a good thing for her." He added.

"How can you say that?" Miranda said sharply.

"Listen." He turned her face toward them. You could hear them giggling. "Look at them. This is the way they both wanted it to be, but they were too stubborn to admit it. His ex sure didn't mind keeping it that way. Plus, she doesn't remember any of that," Avey said, nodding toward Abigail. He turned her to face him. "Just have patience. It will all work out."

"I see your point. Though I may never have my friend back totally, at least, I have her. I do like her spunk," she smiled. "You may be right." She splashed him with a wave of water.

"Don't you know by now, I am always right," he teased back, tossing a large wave of water at her. They all enjoyed the pool a little longer until Scottie could see that Abigail was shivering.

"It is getting cold. Do you want to go up by the fire?" Scottie asked.

"Sure." She answered.

"Hey, do you kids want to stop horse-playing and go chill by the fire?" He called out to Miranda and Avey who were splashing down at the end of the pool.

"S'mores sounds great," Avey said, splashing Miranda one last time.

They all climbed out of the pool and grabbed their towels that were laying on one of the lounge chairs. Once they all had tied their towels around them, they went to the bar and stacked their plates with all the items to make s'mores. Scottie and Abigail sat down on one of the patio sofas next to one another. He picked up one of the roasting forks and placed two of Abigail's marshmallows to roast over the fire. He looked back and gave her a wink. She returned with a smile. *How could I ever forget him? I was crazy not to make him mine. I* won't *make that mistake again if ever given the chance,* she thought to herself. Scottie turned back to watch her marshmallows to make sure not to burn them. They all finished their s'mores.

"I think I am going to put on some dry, warm clothes," Abigail said. "Miranda, you wanna come?"

"That is a great idea. We will be right back." Miranda agreed.

"We are next," Avey called out. He waited till the girls were in the game room. "What is going on with you two?"

"I am not sure. She is so different. Have you noticed?" he asked, leaning back in his seat. He propped his left leg over his right knee.

"I told Miranda the same thing earlier," Avey answered. "But I am asking what is going on between the two of you?"

"I don't know honestly. I have held back my feelings for her for so long. When the accident happened, I feared I had lost the chance. Then I broke up with Amy and said I would tell her as soon as she came out of the coma, but then she didn't remember us. I kind of lost all hope of that ever happening," Scottie paused and clasped his hands together. "But then today she started flirting with me, and the way she looks into my eyes, almost like she is reading my soul."

"We all knew there was chemistry between you two for a long time. Maybe a higher power intervened to make you two see it like everyone else." Avey stated.

Scottie let out a chuckle. "A higher power?"

"Yes, your creator saw how stubborn you two were being and intervened." He added.

"Maybe he could've done that without almost taking her away," Scottie said in a loud, sharp tone.

"Look, I am not trying to upset you. He doesn't do things our way. His thoughts aren't our thoughts, but everything he does is for our good." Avey stated.

"For the good?" He sat up abruptly with both feet on the ground, and his elbows on his knees. "I didn't see any good when she was laid up in that bed," he said in an outburst.

"Let me finish. Listen, of course, what happened to her wasn't good, and we all were destroyed when we found out she didn't know us anymore. But she is still with us. Y'all have been given a second chance. No, she isn't the same Abigail that we all grew up with, but y'all will get to know each other all over again. Without all the stubbornness and denying your true feelings for one another. The chemistry is still there and is a fresh new beginning for you two." He explained.

"What if she never remembers?" Scottie inquired.

"Then we will remember them for her. We can share all our stories with her." He placed his hand on his shoulder. Avey went on.

"I see what you are saying. I just hope she loves me as much as I love her." Scottie said.

"I know. Just remember what I said here tonight. Be patient with her," Avey encouraged.

Mr. Arnold and Mrs. Mia came out. "Is everything okay?" she asked.

"We thought we heard shouting a little while ago," Mr. Arnold stated.

"Oh sorry. We were just cutting up," Avey said as he padded Scottie on the back.

They took a seat on the sofa bench opposite the fire from the boys.

"No worries. Y'all have fun," Mr. Arnold said.

"May I ask y'all a question while Abby isn't around?" Scottie asked.

They both looked puzzled at one another and looked back at him. "Ask away," Mr. Arnold said.

"How do I ask this?" Scottie said.

They gazed over to Avey as if to say what was going on, but he shrugged his shoulders because he had no idea himself what Scottie was trying to ask.

"It's okay, son. You can ask us anything," Mr. Arnold assured.

Scottie nodded and continued. "I have been so stubborn not to tell Abby how I truly feel about her. Today is like a fresh new beginning with her, and I wanted to ask for your permission to date Abby. If not…"

"Son, look at me," Mr. Arnold interrupted, "I think I speak for both of us when I say that you are like our son. We would not wish her to be with anyone else. Of course, you have our permission."

Scottie jumped to his feet and ran over and hugged them both. Mrs. Mia had tears in her eyes. "When do you plan on asking her?" she asked.

"I am not sure. I think tonight would be too fast. Maybe we could go bowling or something tomorrow, or I could take her to her favorite places that we used to go to."

"That sounds like a great idea," Mrs. Mia said.

# CHAPTER 19

## I Always Have Been, and I Always Will Be

Miranda was waiting for Abigail to finish getting dressed. "I can't believe this is finally going to happen," she said, as she sat on Abigail's bed.

"I still can't believe he asked me to go out with him tonight. I just hope he understood when I asked if you and Avey could tag along."

"We are always together, and we have waited for this for so long that it is only fair that we tag along tonight."

"That does seem fair right," Abigail said, turning to face Miranda while she brushed her hair. "I just don't want him to think I don't trust him, because I do."

"I am sure he understands, and he is okay with bringing along his wingman," Miranda said.

"Wingman?" Abigail asked as she turned toward her vanity mirror to add the finishing touches to her hair.

"Yeah, you know like Goose and Maverick in 'Top Gun'." Miranda explained.

"I don't think I remember that movie." She said.

"Well, then I know what we are watching tonight," she said. "Any way, guys like to bring along their best friend on dates, to feed off one another's testosterone or male ego I should say. They call them their wingman. It's a guy thing." Miranda added.

"Okay, I am all done. How do I look?" she asked, standing up in a pose.

"Beautiful as always." Miranda complimented.

"Let's go downstairs and wait for them." Abigail said.

"No, we are going to make this an official date," Miranda said, grabbing her by the wrist.

"What do you mean by that?" She asked.

"Guys are used to waiting on us to finish getting ready for them. So, we are going to hang up here until they arrive." Miranda stated.

"Okay, if you are sure this won't make them mad." She added.

"Please, Amy used to make him wait for hours. I am sure he won't mind waiting a few minutes for you." Miranda continued.

"Hours?" Abigail asked and sat down on the bed.

"Yes. On prom night, he had to wait for almost three hours for her. She almost made us late for our dinner reservation. Luckily, Scottie told her we had to be there almost five hours earlier just so we could make it on time," Miranda explained. "Needless to say, he was already pretty mad by the time we got to the restaurant."

"I can imagine," Abigail said. "I would never treat him like that."

"We all know," Miranda said, "that is why you two are made for one another."

The doorbell rang, and it startled Abigail. She jumped up, "they are here."

"Yes, calm down. Take a deep breath," Miranda said. "Remember you are worth waiting for."

Mr. Arnold called up the stairs, "Girls, your dates are here."

"Be right there." The girls answered.

"Oh my, the butterflies are back again." Abigail said.

"That is a good sign," she said, applying one more coat of her lipstick. "Okay, are you ready?"

"I believe so." Abigail said.

"Lead the way. Tonight is your night," she said as she opened the bedroom door for her.

Abigail headed down the hall to the stairs. As she came down the stairs, Scottie was standing at the door. He was dressed in a black, white, and gray plaid shirt over a solid, white t-shirt, with a pair of black relaxed-fit jeans that had small tears in them. He ran his hands through his curls that were styled but not so much that you couldn't run your hands through them. She took his breath away in her light blue sundress with white daisies. The ruffled hem hit her right below the knee. She had on a light blue jean jacket that looked stone-washed with holes. She rolled the wrist up without it buttoned. *She is so beautiful,* he thought, watching her come down the stairs. As she reached the bottom of the stairs, she could smell his cologne, and it almost stunned her right there on the last step, but he saved her by stretching out his right hand to assist her down.

"Hello," she said with a smile. "You look very nice."

"You are beautiful," he said.

"Thank you. I just threw something on," she smirked.

"You could come in your pajamas, and you would still be stunning," Scottie said.

"Oh, let me pass, please. You two are going to make me vomit before the night is over," Miranda said jokingly as she pushed by them to hug Avey.

"Can I get a photo please?" Mrs. Mia asked.

"Sure, another to add to our binder," Abigail said.

"For sure," Miranda said.

They walked into the living room and stood in front of the famous fireplace backdrop for all the photos. Miranda and Abigail stood in the middle, with Scottie and Avey on each end. "Say cheese," Mrs. Mia said. "CHEESE!" they said in unison.

"Oh, that is a good one for sure," Mr. Arnold said.

"Can you please text it to me, Mom," Abigail said.

"I sure can," Mrs. Mia answered.

"We need to get going," Scottie said. "I am sorry for the rush."

"No, we understand. You have places to be," Mr. Arnold winked. "Y'all be safe and have fun."

"Yes sir," they called out as they headed for the door.

They escorted the girls out to the car. Abigail slipped her hand into Scottie's. He looked down and smiled at her. Then he brought it to his lips and lightly kissed her hand. Chills ran down her spine. *This is going to be a great night,* she thought to herself. He opened the passenger door to his car and shut it once she was in.

"Oh, my. They have already started with the mushy stuff," Miranda said.

"Would you like me to get your door for you, my dear?" Avey asked in a joking tone.

"No. I can get it myself," Miranda answered. She nudged him and opened her car door.

"So where are we headed?" Abigail asked as they backed out of the driveway.

"I want to take you to some of your favorite places," Scottie answered.

"Oh, this will be interesting since I don't remember any of them," she said.

"It's okay. Just pretend you are a tourist and we are taking you out on the town," Avey said.

"It will be fun to get my first experiences with you guys," she said.

"So where are we going first?" Miranda asked.

"I thought a bite to eat would be good to start with," Scottie said. "Maple Street Biscuits Company."

"Oh yes, I can get myself a caramel toffee latte, and the sweet Grace waffles," Miranda said.

"Maybe it will help you sweeten up," Avey teased.

"You better watch yourself,' Miranda said.

Scottie placed his elbow on the console between them and held out his hand for Abigail. She clasped his hand in hers. They stayed that way until they pulled up to Maple Street Biscuits. He raced around the car to prevent Abigail from opening her door.

"You don't have to do that," she told him when he helped her out.

"I know, but I enjoy treating you like the princess you are," he said, smiling at her.

"Well, I could get spoiled if you keep it up," she said.

"Maybe that is what I want to do," he winked as he opened the door to the building.

"Oh boy. I am going to need earplugs, if this is what I am going to hear all night," Miranda teased.

"You know you like to be spoiled. Just in a different way," Avey said.

"Haha," Miranda said.

"Welcome to Maple Street Biscuits," the hostess greeted them from behind the counter. "Can I take your order?"

Abigail started to look over the menu. "Everything here looks so good. How do I know what to choose?" She asked.

"I can tell you what your favorite was to eat when we would come here," Scottie said.

"Yes, please," she said.

"Your favorite was the squawking goat," he said.

"You're pulling my leg," she laughed.

"No, I am serious. Am I right, Miranda?" he asked.

"He is right, that was your favorite," she said.

"Well then, that is what I will have then. The squawking goat," she told the hostess.

"We must have come here a lot if y'all aren't looking at the menu." Abigail said.

"Yeah, we pretty much eat the same thing every time," Miranda said while Scottie was placing his order.

"We are taking your favorite songs tonight to call out when your order is ready. What would you like to put down for your favorite song?" The hostess asked.

"Enchanted," Scottie answered. Abigail looked up at him.

"Are you a Swiftie too?" She teased.

He smirked, and said, "Only when I am with you."

"Please don't be in love with someone else," Abigail quoted.

Scottie replied, "Please don't have someone waiting on you." He pulled out his wallet to pay the hostess. Without taking his gaze from hers. She smiled and nudged his elbow.

"Ugh, that's enough. Can you please just pay already, so we can place our order now?" Miranda spoke in a tone of disgust.

Avey grinned, turning in a full 360 spin, "Ne-e-ar, fa-a-r, wh-e-erever you–"

"Don't start," Miranda interrupted, putting her hand in Avey's face as he started to sing to her. The hostess behind the counter lost it, and she started to laugh. Avey put on a fake frown, "She broke my heart when she said I couldn't sing..." Miranda gave him a look of enough, and he grabbed and hugged her. "Okay, I am just playing, sweetie." They placed their order.

"How will you be paying tonight," the hostess asked.

"Oh, after all that dissing I just got, we are going Dutch," Avey joked. Miranda jabbed him in the side with her left elbow. "Aww, alright, alright. I take that back, we are on the same ticket," he said, messaging his ribs that were now throbbing from her jab. "Man, that hurts."

"You better treat this one right, or she is going to keep you in line," the hostess laughed. "I guess I don't need to ask you for your favorite song." She smiled.

"Please no, don't get him started again," Miranda said.

"Y'all are such a cute couple," she said.

"See, at least someone thinks I am cute," Avey teased as he pulled his wallet out to pay the hostess.

"No, no. She didn't call you cute. She said we are a cute couple. You can't have the cute without me in that conversation, so in all honesty, you are wrong. No one thinks you are cute," Miranda teased.

"What? You don't think I am cute?" he asked as he placed his wallet back in his pocket.

"Hmm, maybe a little." She teased as she grabbed her cup and walked toward the drink station.

"That is just wrong," he said, shaking his hand. He grabbed his cup off the counter and followed her.

After filling their drinks, they went upstairs to sit in their hang-out spot. They were all laughing and carrying on when the manager, Jamie, came up to the table. "I am getting complaints of a group of kids making too much noise," she said.

"We are sorry, Jamie. I am trying to control them, but they are acting like they just broke out of the monkey cage at the zoo," Miranda teased.

"Hey, you know you love this monkey face," Avey said, making faces at her. Miranda rolled her eyes.

"Looks like you have your hands full with that one," Jamie giggled.

"You don't even know half of it," Miranda said.

"Oh my. Abigail, it is so good to see you. It has been a while. How are you doing since your accident?" Jaime asked.

Abigail looked puzzled. "I am sorry, do I know you?"

"Oh my. You poor thing. I am so sorry. I forgot to introduce myself," Jamie said in her southern drawl accent.

"Please don't feel bad, Jamie. This is her first night out since the accident. We are taking her out on the town to show her a good time," Scottie said. "You didn't do anything wrong, and everything is fine. Abby, this is Jamie. She has seen us here so much that she knows us by name," Scottie said, introducing them.

"Oh, hello. It is nice to meet you, again," Abigail smiled.

"Nice to meet you too, dear. Well, I heard the commotion and knew it had to be y'all. I haven't seen y'all in so long, so I wanted to come up and say hi," she looked around the table as if something or someone was missing. "No, Amy tonight I presume? Where is she anyway? I don't believe I have ever seen you here without her?" She asked.

"We are no longer together," he stated as he sat back, and placed his arm on the back of Abigail's chair. The swinging of his arm sent the aroma of his cologne through the air. *Oh, my. He smells so good. His gentle touch puts all my anxious nerves to ease,* she thought to herself.

"Oh, I see," she winked at him. "Good for you! I better get back downstairs. Now don't be strangers," she told them as she walked away.

The guys went and picked up their orders when the song names were called. They sat and visited for a little while after everyone had finished eating.

"Where are we going next?" Abigail smiled. She leaned over and looped her arm in his propped on the table.

"It is a surprise, but I am quite sure you will like it," he assured her.

"Boy, I like surprises, but it is so hard to be patient to wait for them," she giggled. "Thank you so much. This is fun, and we have only been out for an hour."

"It is still young. There is much more to come," he said, smiling at her.

"I am so glad we are back here together," Miranda said. "I haven't been here since…" she paused. She caught what she was about to say and didn't want to bring the night down by discussing the past.

"The accident," Abigail said softly.

"Yes, since the accident," Miranda said.

"It's okay. It is a part of our lives, and we cannot just act like it never happened," she said.

"Trust me, I live with a reminder every day." She pulled back her left sleeve, and her scar was visible on her arm.

"I am sorry, I shouldn't have mentioned it," Miranda said.

"No, it is fine," Abigail said. "As I said, it is a part of our lives now, and we cannot just ignore it. I am glad we can now make new memories. I know they won't replace the old ones, but the new ones aren't so bad," she said, placing her right hand on Scottie's hand.

"I couldn't agree more," he said, smiling at her.

"So y'all didn't get out much after my accident, I am assuming," she asked.

"Not really. We had graduated, so there was no reason to have to get out," Miranda said.

"So, tell me of other places that we would go to hang out and pass the time," Abigail said.

"Well, there was the bowling alley, going to the Tree House to eat some wings, and dance to the live music," Miranda said.

"What? They have places like that here?" She asked.

"Yes, and if I remember correctly, you two caused a crazy commotion the last time y'all went to eat there together," Avey said.

"What? How did that happen? What did we do?" She asked.

"I think that would be better if you told this story," Avey said, looking over to Scottie. Scottie began to stir his iced tea with his straw.

"We danced together, and word got back to Amy. Boy, did that ever blow up in my face," he said.

"You and I have danced before?" Abigail said.

"More than once," Miranda giggled.

"And every time Amy would blow her top," Avey giggled. "Do y'all remember her reaction when Abigail won the prom Queen, and she didn't? Man, she stopped dead in her tracks on the way to the stage when they called your name," Avey laughed.

"She got what she deserved that night," Miranda said.

"What do you mean?" Abigail asked.

"You were crowned queen and Scottie was King of the prom court," Miranda answered.

"Oh my, now I know why she was so furious," she said.

"No. That isn't even the best part," Avey said.

"Why? What else happened?" Abigail asked.

"We had just finished the prom King and Queen dance. We both were thirsty, so we headed to the punch table. Amy was standing with her back turned to us, and I guess she was so mad that she didn't realize the song had ended. You could see the steam coming out of her ears." They all laughed. "When we got to the table to grab a glass of punch, she spun around and bumped into you and her glass of red punch went all over her pink lace dress. As you can imagine, she was furious and she blew her top," he said.

"Oh, my goodness. Well obviously, I wasn't that bad of a person to do something like that on purpose," Abigail said.

"No, not at all," Scottie said.

"I was so proud of you for standing your ground that night. You would normally just back down and let her treat you however she liked, but not that night. I was just mad because I always missed you standing up to her," Miranda said.

"Oh, wow. Is this how all our stories go?" She asked.

"Pretty much," Miranda said.

"Well, I didn't want to go to the prom anyway. Dressed as some penguin in a suit. I sweat so bad that night, I almost dehydrated," Scottie joked. "But one good thing did come from that night."

"What?" Miranda asked.

"I got to dance with the most beautiful girl there," he said and squeezed Abigail's hand.

"No, I think that was me," Avey said, smirking at Miranda.

"Oh, don't you start with the mushy stuff? That is their thing, not ours," Miranda said.

Scottie laughed at them, "It wouldn't hurt for you to be mushier together. I sure don't see anything wrong with it," he teased them.

Avey motioned to his watch to Scottie. Scottie clicked his phone and saw that it was 5:15 PM displayed on his screen.

"We need to get going," Scottie said.

"Oh, onto our next adventure?" Abigail asked.

"That is right," he said with a smile.

A few moments later, Jamie came to check to see if they needed refills.

"We are good. We were about to leave," Scottie said.

"I will get these dishes out of the way then," she said as she started picking up their empty plates. "How did you like it?" She asked as she picked up Abigail's plate.

"It was delicious, I can see why it is my favorite. The sauce is amazing," she said.

"Thank you, I will let the chef know. Don't be a stranger, now. Come back and see me soon," she said as she balanced their plates and returned to the kitchen.

Everyone grabbed their stuff and headed to the car. Scottie once again opened the door for Abigail and shut it when she was in. They drove down 810, Islands Expressway. When they came parallel with the ocean, Abigail almost jumped out of her seat.

"Is that the ocean?" she asked with excitement.

"It sure is," Scottie answered.

"Are we going to the beach?" she asked. He didn't answer, instead, he just looked over and winked at her. She leaned over and squeezed his arm.

They drove for fifteen more minutes and pulled in at Ben and Jerry's ice cream shop.

"Ice cream?" She said with a big smile. "Oh, I love ice cream."

"I know, and you love Ben and Jerry's," he said as he got out to open her door.

"This is an amazing night," she said.

"This best is yet to come," he smiled.

She looked over the menu while they waited in line. "Hmm, there are so many good things to choose from. How do I pick what I want?" she said, tapping her finger on her chin.

"Order whatever you like," Scottie said.

"Hello, can I help you?" The young girl in the window asked.

"Umm, yes, is there a way that I can have three different scoops of ice cream?" Abigail asked.

"Sure," the young girl said. "Would you like it in a regular cone or waffle cone?" she asked.

"I would like to try the waffle cone," Abigail answered.

"What three scoops would you like?" the young girl asked.

"I would like the Coffee, Coffee BuzzBuzzBuzzBuzz! in the bottom of the cone, regular vanilla in the middle, and Butter Pecan on top," she answered.

"Will that be all?" She asked.

Abigail stepped aside for Scottie to give his order. "I would just like a small regular cone of the Mint Chocolate Chunk, and that will be all for our order," he said as he pulled out his wallet to pay.

"What are you getting, Miranda?" She asked.

"I believe Avey and I are going to share a large cone of Chocolate Peanut Butter Swirl," she answered.

"Oh, that sounds so good too. There are too many to choose from," Abigail said.

"We can keep coming back until you try them all," Scottie said.

"You promise?" Abigail asked.

"I promise," he said. *She agreed to several more dates,* he thought to himself. He turned and winked at Avey, and he gave him a thumbs up.

"What are you two up to?" Miranda answered.

"You will just have to wait and see," he answered without looking at her. He knew if he looked, she would give him irresistible puppy eyes. "Not going to happen," he said.

"Come on, at least a hint," she begged.

"Nope, but don't worry, it won't be much longer," he teased as he reached to pull out his wallet to pay. He placed their order once it was their turn.

They all got back into the car, and Scottie drove to the end of Tybrisa Street and turned right into the Tybee Beach Parking Lot. He found a parking spot, and rushed around to open the door for Abigail. They grabbed their bags and made their way to the beach. The sun was starting to set. *Everything is working out perfectly. Hopefully, all will go well from here,* he thought to himself.

"Blankets?" Abigail asked.

"Yes, you love sunsets, so I thought it would be good to see one tonight," he explained.

"You are spoiling me," she teased.

"That is kind of the point," he said.

The beach wasn't too crowded now that the sun was setting. Scottie picked a quiet spot away from everyone. Avey and Miranda took a blanket and sat not too far from them.

"Now can you please tell me what you two are up to?" Miranda asked.

"Patience is a virtue," he whispered and kissed her on the forehead.

"I hate that quote," she told him with a frown.

"It will be worth the wait, I promise," he assured her.

"Ice cream and the sunset on a beach with you. It can't get any more perfect than this," Abigail said. The sky was full of dark pink and purple colors, with the pretty orange and yellows close to the horizon where the sun was setting. It was a breathtaking view. *I hope it can,* he thought to himself. He opened his phone to his camera. They snuggled close, and he raised his cell phone high to catch the sunset behind them. “Perfect,” she said as she looked at the photo they had taken.

“Yes, you are,” he said with a smile.

“Not all of me,” she said, rubbing her left arm.

“You are perfect in my eyes. You don’t have one part of you that I don’t love...” he paused. *Did I just say that out loud? Did I just tell her I love her?* His heart began to race.

“Abby, I’m sorry. That just came out. I should have told you that years ago, but I was too much of a coward. I was too scared I would lose you altogether. I have that same fear even now, but I have to get this off my chest. I have carried the weight too long, and if you don’t feel the same I understand.” She started to speak, but he placed his finger over her lips. “Please let me finish. I was so scared to come yesterday because I wasn’t sure how you would react to me. When you started flirting with me….”

“I flirted with you?” She teased. He looked at her as if to say please let me finish. “Oh, I’m sorry. Please finish.”

“I want to spoil you and give you the world. Abby Whittinger, will you make it official and be my girl?”

Their eyes met, and she softly said “Oh, Scottie. Don’t you know? I always have been, and I always will be.”

# ACKNOWLEDGMENTS

I want to thank God for directing my path through the open doors He provided to make this dream come true.

Thank you to the reader. You are the reason I am a writer. I pray this book inspires you to follow along on the adventures that are sure to follow.

I am grateful for everyone at Purpose Media Publishing and the opportunity to work beside each of you from getting the process of publishing started to the printing. Donnie Copeland, you encouraged me and gave me hope from our first conversation to not only to publish this book, but to continue the dream of being an author. Shannon at Speak Beautiful, thank you for working with me to iron out all the flaws. Turning it into the finished project from the manuscript to my art work for the book cover.. I look forward to working with you on many more.. Robyn – it was a pleasure working with you to make sure that everything was just right from the cover to the back of the book. Thank you for your patience with me through this journey. Thank you to all of you for assisting me whether big or small to making my dream come true of not only holding the printed copy, but also having it available for readers in many formats.

To my wild and crazy family, you are a BIG part of my life. Each of you holds a special place in my heart. I will cherish all the colorful and unforgettable memories with each of you forever. Uncle Ricky Mobley – I wish you were here to be with me on my journey in the publishing world, but I will carry your memory, smile, and unique laughter with me every day. Uncle Duane Hearold – Thank you for the introduction to Purpose Media

Publishing. Without your thoughtful suggestion and introduction, my dream would not be a reality.

To my wacky and lovable pack of four. You inspire me every day to be better than I was the day before. I am thankful God blessed me to be your mom. Each of you, in your own unique way make our chaotic, stressful, loud, messy place a home that is filled with love and laughter. Y'all have supported me in many ways through this remarkable journey and encouraged me when I wanted to give up. I am thankful for your thoughts, advice, input, ideas, and lending your ears to listen to the chapters come together. I love all four of you three thousand.

To all the remarkable artists from REO Speedway, Ed Sheeran, Bruno Mars, One Direction, Taylor Swift, and so many more, who string our hearts and get us through the hardest, saddest, happiest, and love-struck moments of our lives. THANK YOU for the influence your music has had on my life from a very young age. It can take me back to a time in my past just by the first line in a song. Therefore, I wanted to share a playlist with the reader of some songs that can connect you throughout the chapters of Scottie and Abigail's story. May they bring you back to them in an instant as so many do for me.

# Scottie & Abigail's Playlist

1. Always Be Together – Little Mix
2. Don't You Forget About Me – Simple Minds
3. It's Nice to Have a Friend – Taylor Swift
4. My Person – Spencer Crandall
5. The Boy is Mine – Brandy & Monica
6. More than Friends – Jason Mraz (feat. Meghan Trainer)
7. You're the One I Want – John Travolta & Olivia Newton John (Grease Soundtrack)
8. One Call Away – Charlie Puth
9. Graduation (Friends Forever) - Vitamin C
10. You are the Reason – Calum Scott
11. Beautiful Things – Benson Boone
12. In Case You Didn't Know - Brett Young
13. What-Ifs - Kane Brown (feat. Lauren Alaina)
14. Gift of a Friend - Demi Lovato
15. Photograph - Ed Sheeran
16. Count on Me - Bruno Mars
17. I Found the Answer in You – Loving Caliber & Mia Niles
18. Friendship? Jordy Searcy
19. Enchanted – Taylor Swift
20. One Thing – One Direction
21. You Belong to Me – Taylor Swift
22. Thinking Out Loud – Ed Sheeran
23. Story of My Life – One Direction
24. All the Girl's You've Loved Before – Taylor Swift
25. Until I Found You – Stephen Sanchez
26. Lover – Taylor Swift

*Listen To the Playlist on:*

# ABOUT THE AUTHOR

Alisha Stutson is a wife, mother of four, and an author. She lives in central Louisiana where she grew up picking wildflowers, sucking on wild honeysuckles, eating crawfish, and going to church. Her debut novel *I Always Have, and I Always Will* came to her in a dream in 2020. When she is not writing or listening to audio books, she spends time with her family fishing, watching crime shows, and listening to podcasts.

www.ingramcontent.com/pod-product-compliance
Lightning Source LLC
LaVergne TN
LVHW020713110826
845149LV00012B/2238

* 9 7 9 8 9 9 0 0 8 9 5 1 8 *